THE LAST STAND

Kevin O'Hagan

**Grosvenor House
Publishing Limited**

This book is published by
Grosvenor House Publishing Ltd
Link House
140 The Broadway, Tolworth, Surrey, KT6 7HT.
www.grosvenorhousepublishing.co.uk

This book is a work of fiction. Any resemblance to
people or events, past or present, is purely coincidental.

A CIP record for this book
is available from the British Library

ISBN 978-1-83975-212-4

Dedication

For all the incredible NHS staff who fought the
coronavirus. God bless you all.

Other Books by the Author

Battlescars

No Hiding Place

Acknowledgements

Because of the coronavirus, the writing of this book has been very much a solo project. The worldwide web has been a good friend and companion to me, providing me with the much-needed references and little nuggets of knowledge when required.

Many thanks as always to my daughter Lauren for proofreading the manuscript and lending her professional advice and knowledge.

Thanks to my son Tom for the book cover design work.

Thanks to my brothers and sisters in the martial arts and military world for giving me inspiration and reference where needed.

Thank you also to the many great authors out there who inspire and push me to become a better writer every time I open my laptop and hit the keys. I salute you all.

Thanks once again to my publishers, Grosvenor House.

Finally, thanks to all my family for your love and support.

Author's note

The cities, towns and locations in this novel exist in real life. I grew up in many of them. I have taken the cheeky liberty of changing many names and places to suit this story. Landscapes, businesses, streets, and layouts take on another imaginary life. All the characters are pure fiction. Thank you for indulging me to help me create this storyline.

Preface

I finished the majority of this book whilst in lockdown during the Covid-19 pandemic. It was a strange and unsettling time, and writing this book became one of my sanctuaries to prevent myself from going stir crazy.

Before the virus, I was at a crossroads where to go with the story, but the enforced isolation kickstarted my creativity and helped me finish the book in record time.

In this period, there was much sadness – not only from the daily reports of so many people dying and ill, but also on a personal level. Writing helped me escape the doom and gloom for a while and got me to focus on something other than the endless news reports.

My daily routines became exercise, writing, reading, playing guitar, and a little meditation.

I self-isolated with my lovely wife Tina, and we grew closer as a result of the experience. However, we both missed personal contact with our children and grand-children.

As I am writing this, things are beginning to ease a little and there is some light at the end of the tunnel, thank God.

The book you have in your hands is my third novel. It is also the third outing for Tony Slade.

Yes, he is back for another action-packed story with many twists and turns. You just can't keep a good man down, or can you?

So, time to sit back, put your feet up with your favourite drink, and begin the adventure.

God bless you all, and here's to better days ahead.

Kevin
May 2020

Last Stand

Prologue

Gary Carter pulled the hood up on his sweatshirt and then zipped his jacket up to his throat. It was a bitterly cold night.

He took another drag on his cigarette, taking some comfort in the sight of the glowing red ashes. He stole a glance up from the bench he was sat on to look at the digital screen of train arrivals. The time read 10.10pm.

His train was running ten minutes late. No surprise there.

He was waiting at Bristol Temple Meads station in the South West of England.

Why was this island so cold?

Some mumbled message that he just about understood had come over the loudspeaker a few minutes ago, confirming the train's delay.

Carter was alone on the platform, except for one other person. An older man sat on a bench further down the way, intently occupied scrolling on his phone which was attached to earbuds. He was lost in his own space.

During his brief time in the UK, Carter had found that most people were very insulated and did not talk much to visitors. The exact polar opposite to his own country. He felt alone here and out of place.

He had travelled to the United Kingdom recently from America, on a family quest. He was searching for somebody. A man who, up to recently, he did not know existed. An interesting and elusive stranger. His information had told him that the man had been in Bristol, but the trail had gone cold. His other lead was in Wales.

This was the last train running today that would take him to his destination of Cardiff in South Wales, where he hoped the trail would pick up again. It was his last hope of finding the man and fulfilling a promise he had made to his sister.

He took another drag on his cigarette and ran his hand over a week's growth of beard. He mused that it was about time he had a shave and shower. It had been a while. He had let things slip of late.

Carter unzipped the large holdall he had with him and rummaged inside until he found a Snickers bar. He tore off the wrapper and devoured it in three bites. He could not remember when he had last eaten a proper cooked meal.

It had not always been like this. Not when he was in the forces as a US Marine. Discipline was the key and, back then, he'd had that in abundance.

Gary Carter was born and raised in Brooklyn, New York. He had joined the US Marine Corps at twenty years of age, and it had become his life ever since, until a few years ago when he finally came out.

He had seen his fair share of action all over the world in his time. Iraq, Bosnia, and Afghanistan. He had the medals and the scars to prove it. He did not regret a minute of his service.

Since coming out of the Marines, things had not been so good.

He had returned to his home city of New York, but felt like an outsider. So many things had changed since he enlisted. Everyday life was happening around him, but he did not feel part of it. He had been warned about this by other military veterans. They informed him that it was hard to fit back into a society that you had not been part of for so long. There was no sense of belonging. You felt like a square peg in a round hole.

His family did their best to be supportive. His father and mother tried to help him. So did his older sister Ruby. But it just was not enough.

The job front had not been great either. A bit of labouring on a few construction sites had been okay, but the winter months in New York could be harsh, so work of this nature became scarce and he was eventually laid off.

He had tried some security work, but patrolling around Walmart looking out for somebody shoplifting a packet of Oreos or a bottle of Jack Daniels did not quite match up to a firefight in the desert.

His father was Clint Carter, a well-known and respected multimillion-dollar newspaper tycoon and owner of the *Manhattan News*. He had offered him a job at the newspaper on more than one occasion, but it was not for Gary. He could not see himself sitting at a desk tapping on computer keys all day. Plus, he did not want to live in his father's shadow, nor for people to think that he had been given a free handout from his old man when others had worked hard to get a position in the newspaper business.

He did not want his father's charity.

They had fallen out over the issue and argued on many occasions. Both men were stubborn and neither of them could agree.

Gary had ended up working on the doors of clubland in Greenwich Village and the Hell's Kitchen districts of New York.

It had been decent enough work and he had met many men like him. Ex-forces, down on their luck, reduced to using a fraction of their skills to chuck a few drunks out of a drinking establishment at the end of a night.

All had been okay until the incident.

One Friday night, Carter had refused a right pair of 'muppets' entry into the club where he was working. Nothing unusual there. They shouted threats of a comeback as they walked off. Still nothing unusual.

Most did not follow up on their threats, but that night, these two guys came back at closing time and waited for Carter in the parking lot. They set about him with baseball bats.

Gary Carter was more than a match for them. He had always been a right handful when it came to a fight. He had trained in unarmed combat in the army, but had also fought in a dozen or more Muay Thai boxing bouts. He had won most by knockout.

That night in the parking lot, he had hit one guy on the jaw with a left hook so hard that, when he eventually woke up, his clothes were out of fashion.

He disarmed the other guy and smashed his leg with a brutal round kick, before bringing the fight to an end with a crunching rising knee under his chin.

Carter had not waited around to admire his accomplishments. He had jumped into his car and driven away into the night.

When his adrenaline had subsided, he became slightly worried about how hard he had hit both men, but then he rationalised it by telling himself that if he had not done so, he could have been seriously injured himself or even killed.

All seemed okay until the police came knocking at his door the next morning to inform him that he was under arrest.

Apparently, both men he had encountered were in hospital; one was still unconscious. Carter was looking at serious charges, especially if this man did not wake up soon.

Thankfully, the man did regain consciousness, but the case ended up in court.

In a cruel twist of fate, it looked like Gary Carter was going to be incarcerated. But his defence lawyer produced timely last-minute CCTV footage from the incident in the parking lot – whose existence had previously been denied – and the jury deemed that Carter had acted in self-defence. Case dismissed.

The whole episode had unnerved Gary. He knew deep down that he had a violent streak in him that was dangerous when unleashed. He decided that he did not have the temperament for this type of work anymore, so he left.

Gary then spiralled down into depression. He slipped into drinking himself stupid and just lost track of his life.

He left New York and went drifting around America with no purpose. He just about kept his head above water by working cash-in-hand in a host of dead-end labouring jobs that nobody else wanted to do.

He eventually came home to Brooklyn, and one night found himself standing on its famous bridge, staring into the dark, icy, cold waters below. He was contemplating jumping in and ending the pain.

Something then occurred that would make him change his mind and reassess his life.

His phone had rung.

It did not ring too often these days, and when it did, he normally did not answer. But for some reason that night, he fished it out of his pocket and looked at the caller ID. It was his big sister Ruby. They had not spoken in a while.

When he answered, she explained that she had been trying to get hold of him for days. She went on to tell him that both their father and mother had been rushed into hospital a week ago after their car had swerved to avoid another car coming on the wrong side of a dark road in Woodland, Burlington County, New Jersey. They had lost control of their vehicle and driven headlong into a tree. They had been returning home from a weekend break.

It was found out later that the other car had been stolen by joyriders and eventually abandoned.

Both their parents sustained serious head and spinal injuries. The driver, Clint Carter, had come off the worst of the two.

At present, their father was on a life support system in a deep coma. The doctors had informed Ruby that, due to the severity of his injuries, he was totally unresponsive, and the life support machine was basically keeping him alive. If he showed no immediate improvement, a decision would soon have to be made on the best course of action to take. The clock was ticking on whether to switch off the machine which was keeping him breathing.

Katy Carter, their mother, was conscious but very poorly. When she was finally a bit stronger, she had been informed of her husband's condition. She had asked for her children to be there when the decision to switch off the life support machine was to be made.

That time had arrived.

Ruby asked Gary to come to the hospital. This shook him out of his dark thoughts and he immediately said that he would.

Katy was getting a little stronger every day, but she still remained in ICU.

When Ruby and Gary were finally united with their mother, they collectively had a grave decision to make.

The doctors had informed them that even if Clint somehow miraculously came out of the coma, he would be paralysed from the neck down and severely brain-damaged.

Clint Carter was a proud man. An active man in his prime. Day-to-day, he was very much hands-on with the newspaper. He would not want to end up the way the doctors had described.

After some agonising, the family decided that the best thing for everybody was to let him go. So, Clint's life tragically ended at the age of sixty-two.

Gary's mother Katy was devastated.

The funeral was a big affair. Clint Carter was an important name in the circles of the rich and famous in New York. His untimely death was splashed across the front pages of every tabloid, including his own.

The Mayor of New York, and even the President himself, heaped praise on the man who, through his newspaper, had waged a war on crime and drug use on the streets of the city. He had been instrumental in what was to be called the 'Great Clean-Up' – a joint scheme between Carter and the Mayor to drop the crime statistics in New York, which they achieved convincingly.

This powerful, charitable, and well-liked man would be sadly missed in the New York community.

Katy had been too ill to attend the funeral and far too fragile to deal with the circumstances. As far as her health went, the doctors did not know if she would ever walk again or have any lasting neurological damage. It was still too soon to say.

A few days after the funeral, Katy took a turn for the worse, catching a chest infection. Both Ruby and Gary immediately rushed to her bedside. The thought of also losing their mother was unconceivable.

Katy was conscious and using a nasal cannula to administer oxygen to aid her breathing. She was pleased to see them, but she also seemed agitated. She beckoned them closer to her bedside.

She told them that she had come to a decision and needed to disclose a secret to them both. It was a secret that she had kept buried for a long time and had agonised for years over whether to reveal it or not. But now, in her present condition and with the passing of her husband, her future was uncertain, so she wanted to unburden herself to her children. Ruby and Gary wondered what on earth was coming now.

Katy told them that Clint had been a wonderful husband and she had been faithful to him her whole married life. There had never been nobody else. Their father had truly been a special person. But there had been another man she had been with when she was just a young girl, when her name was Katy Connor. He had featured prominently in her life at that time and still did, due to reasons she was about to disclose.

Katy had been born and bred in Durham in England, and that was where she met this man. At the time, he was no more than a boy, really, and they had gone out for some while. He had treated her like a princess and, although both of them had been young, she felt that they had loved each other.

Their relationship had been blossoming until an incident changed everything, and it had all unravelled. Katy was the one who finished it.

This boy had a violent streak in him. It had been a product of a tough upbringing. He had never been violent to her, but that one night, she had seen a dark side to his character that had shocked her deeply. For a moment, she had looked into his eyes, and what she saw there frightened her.

She had been heartbroken, but she had stuck to her guns even though it hurt her deeply, especially when he had come to her house pleading with her mother to talk to her. She never did.

Soon after this, she learnt that he had joined the army and was gone out of her life for good.

Katy eventually went on to meet Clint, but she never forgot the boy.

Ruby and Gary were puzzled why their mother was telling them this. It was obviously painful for her to dig up these memories. Finally, Katy went on to drop a bombshell on both of them with the rest of the story.

A few years later, she had quite by chance run into this person again in a local nightclub where they both used to go to when they were together. He had been home on leave from the army. She was out celebrating a work colleague's new promotion, and it was the first time she had set foot in the club for some while. Clubbing no longer held any interest for her.

They had both got talking about old times. A lot of water had gone under the bridge by then, but it seemed in some ways as if they had never been apart. Both shared a few drinks and a few stories. They felt easy in each other's company. They agreed to leave the past in the past.

One thing led to another and they ended up at her flat, where they slept together.

The next day, they realised it had been a terrible mistake, especially Katy, as she was engaged to Clint at that time. So, once again, they went their separate ways. Katy was riddled with guilt for the moment of weakness, but to make matters more complicated, a few weeks later Katy found out that she was pregnant.

She was terrified. She had a good relationship with Clint, and they were planning on emigrating to his home country of the USA and getting married.

She knew the other man was travelling the world in the army, and it would be futile to try and contact him and tell him that he was going to be the father of her child. There was no point, and it would have spoiled everything. Her future was with Clint. She knew this, so she decided not to say anything and let Clint believe he was the father. She knew that he could provide a much more stable upbringing for her unborn child.

Clint was over the moon. He had no reason not to doubt that it was his child. They moved back to his home city of New York and married immediately.

Soon the baby was born. A healthy 8lb girl. They named her Ruby.

Katy had started a new life for herself thousands of miles away from the one in England; a comfortable and lucrative one. Clint moved up through the inner circles of the newspaper world to end up owning the *Manhattan News*. Katy had wanted for nothing. She had gone on to have an incredibly happy and successful marriage with Clint, especially when their son Gary came along a little later.

However, some nights when Clint was working late, she lay in bed on her own and her thoughts would drift back to her times in England and the boy she gave up. She wondered where he had ended up. She also wondered if he was still alive.

Katy had been harbouring the secret for a long time. Sometimes the guilt had become unbearable. But now, after the recent tragic events, she felt the time was right to reveal the secret and clear her conscience, for better or worse. She feared that if she did not get any better and pass away, then the secret would die with her.

She had been brought up a devout Catholic and she needed to confess her indiscretion before it was too late. She confessed that Ruby's biological father was a man by the name of Tony Slade.

Ruby was shellshocked. Clint had always been her dad, and she'd had no reason to think otherwise. Now, her mother's revelation had turned her world upside down.

When her mother had first disclosed the secret to her, she went through the whole gamut of emotions. There had been total disbelief, then anger towards her mother. Next, the tears came, followed eventually by the cold hard realisation that she did not really know who she was.

Ruby told her mother that Katy might feel unburdened now, but it had opened up a whole can of worms for *her*. She had stormed out the hospital with Gary in pursuit, trying to pacify her.

For days, she tried to process this information and did some serious soul-searching. She could ignore the revelation and just get on with her life, but the seed had been planted.

Ruby was a tenacious character. She knew that, deep down, she could not let it lie. Finally, she decided that now she knew the truth, she needed to trace her biological father.

In the eyes of the public and the working environment, Clint Carter would always be her dad, but for her own personal peace of mind, she needed to find this man. Just as she had not known until this moment that he existed, likewise this man had no idea that he had fathered a child. What the hell would his reaction be if they met? Would he even want to know her?

Ruby eventually spoke at length to her mother and made peace. Through a lot of tears and emotion, Katy agreed that if Ruby wanted to, she should seek out Tony Slade.

Katy told her that she had no idea where he may be or if, indeed, he was alive. He had spent most of his life in the army, so it might be impossible to find him. He could be anywhere. But in these days of the internet, Ruby was confident that she could unearth some sort of lead to him.

According to Katy, if he had survived his career in the military, he may well have gone back to his home city of Newcastle or to nearby Durham at some time, and that might be a good starting point.

Ruby knew she could do the detective work on the computer, but she would not have the time to visit the UK. Not now that she going to have to step up to run Clint Carter's business as he had always wanted her to do.

She needed to be here in Brooklyn to deal with the legal aspects of this and to oversee how the firm was going to proceed. She also needed to be close to her mother and, if possible, help her back to health and to get over her terrible loss. So, she asked Gary if he would help her find this man.

At first, he had been against it. He was also finding it hard to comprehend that Ruby and he had different fathers. But finally, his own curiosity got the better of him.

He had agreed. He wanted to help his sister, but it would also give him some purpose in his life again. Being an ex-military man himself just might be the edge he needed to help track this Tony Slade down. This ultimately had brought Gary Carter to the UK in his search.

He and Ruby had dug around on the internet before he left. Randomly, they thought they would type the name Tony Slade into Google, and had been surprised to come up with a score of hits and some interesting news from recent times about him.

He indeed had been ex-military and had had a successful career. Recently, though, he had been involved in a big newsworthy incident. Apparently, Tony Slade had survived what was being called the 'Coffee Shop Massacre' in a city called Bristol in the South West of England.

It had been some sort of random mass shooting. Ruby told Gary that she could remember reading a small news item in the *Manhattan News* about this, but at that time, she obviously had no reason to make a connection.

The newspaper article went on to say that he was alive but currently unconscious after being shot three times. He was in a Bristol hospital. The police desperately wanted to question him. He apparently faced some serious allegations.

They both regarded a grainy image of the man on the computer screen from the article. The photograph had been taken many years ago and showed Tony Slade as a young man dressed in full paratrooper uniform.

They had tentatively found him, but the news item was months old.

They searched for more news. The last piece they found was about his disappearance from the hospital. Police had a slim belief that he may have slipped over the bridge into Wales, but any other leads were sketchy.

This had set Gary on his way.

He arrived in England safely and took a National Express coach from London Heathrow Airport to Bristol. Things were shaping up well until his luck ran out when he tracked down the hospital in Bristol where Slade had been admitted. He was told that Slade had gone outside in a wheelchair for some air with the help of a visiting friend and, to all intents and purposes, had disappeared. They knew nothing else.

He hung around Bristol for a few days and finally got another break when Ruby contacted him to say that she had discovered a recent major newspaper piece online about Slade. It had appeared in a local Bristol newspaper called *West Country Express*, written by a Susie Rawlings. Apparently, the police had finally tracked Slade to an island off the Bristol Channel named Graig O Mor, where he had been hiding out.

There had been another major shootout and, once again, Slade had escaped, airlifted out of the sea by a mystery helicopter. His whereabouts were still unknown.

Gary had thanked Ruby and told her he would see what he could dig up. The more he found out about this Tony Slade, the more it intrigued him. This guy was turning out to be Billy the Kid!

Gary went to the offices of the *West Country Express* to look for Susie Rawlings, the writer of the article. He was told by her colleagues that she no longer worked there and had moved to London after being offered a job by the mainstream tabloid *The Daily News*.

A man called Matt Sloan said that if he left his mobile number with him, he would give her a ring. Gary gave it to him. The man also asked what he wanted her for, but Gary declined to tell him.

Gary decided he would not hold his breath on getting a phone call back, as the man seemed more interested in stuffing the last remnants of a pizza in his mouth and slurping on a bottle of Pepsi.

Frustrated by the news, he decided to go to Cardiff and get a boat trip over to the island of Graig O Mor to find out a bit more about the incident that had happened there. He had nothing else to go on.

One thing he was sure of: Gary and this man Slade had a lot in common.

Gary Carter's thoughts returned to the present as he became aware that somebody else had come onto the station platform. Even with his eyes shut, he knew. Call it a sixth sense. Call it his army training. Either way, he felt it.

He slowly opened his eyes and observed that the newcomers were a young teenage couple who were now sitting on the bench next to him. They were giggling, sharing some private joke. They then briefly kissed and cuddled. They looked like they had enjoyed a good evening out somewhere.

It made Carter think about the fact that he had never really been in a serious relationship with any girl. He did not really know what it was like to be young and in love, with the whole world ahead of you. Making plans, enjoying each other's company. He smiled grimly to himself.

The Marines had been his girlfriend, wife, and mistress.

He slipped back to his thoughts.

Another chilled blast of wind shot up from the platform. It was a bleak February night. It had rained most of the day. Winter wasn't quite ready to release its icy grip on the UK just yet.

Coming from New York, he was no stranger to cold weather, but this somehow felt different. Maybe he was finally going soft.

He stubbed out his last cigarette, which he had bummed off a stranger earlier. He folded his arms tightly around himself and sank further down the bench.

His breath tasted sour from whisky and coffee. He was down to the last of his money, which Ruby had given him along with flight tickets. How the fuck had he fallen so far?

Tiredness suddenly came over him and he closed his eyes for a moment. Another muffled announcement informed that the train would be delayed ten more minutes.

As he mused on these thoughts, the quiet was shattered by loud, raucous voices, as three youths spilled onto the platform, all of them drunk or high, and extremely animated.

Carter regarded them impassively. They seemed to be carbon copies of most other youths he was used to seeing these days, whether it be in the States or here in the UK. The dress code was hoodies, baseball caps, and jeans pulled low on their hips.

Attitude and swagger went hand-in-hand with their gangster image. He estimated they were between seventeen and twenty years of age. The largest of the three was wearing a white baseball cap and a large gold chain around his neck.

The big lad scanned the platform and his gaze landed on the young couple. He nudged the other two with him. Carter sensed these boys were looking for trouble and a suitable victim. In this case, two victims: the boy and the girl.

He watched the scenario unfold and slid slightly back up on his bench.

He could smell trouble a mile away. That is what had made him a good soldier. A bloody good soldier!

Gold Chain, Zit Boy, and Goatee – as Carter had decided to christen them – swaggered up to the couple, who visibly flinched when they got close.

'This is your girlfriend, is it?' Gold Chain aggressively asked the boy.

'Yes,' he replied.

Gold Chain regarded the girl.

'What are you doing with a wanker like this, love? You need a real man, darling.'

As he said this, he rubbed his crotch suggestively. Gold Chain looked around at his two cronies, who both sniggered.

'Don't be so immature and go away,' said the girl defiantly.

The boy nervously grabbed the girl's hand and whispered something under his breath to her.

'Fuck you, bitch!' growled Gold Chain.

The boy stood up. 'Look, we don't want any trouble.'

'Well, too bad, dickhead, because you just met it, eh, lads?' replied Gold Chain.

Goatee and Zit Boy moved closer, like a pair of scavenging hyenas.

'We are part of the Ice Squad gang, and here is our calling card.'

Gold Chain pulled a knife from his pocket and snapped it open in front of the boy's face.

'Want some of this, asshole?'

The boy fell back to the bench, his eyes wide with fear. Gold Chain grinned and thrust the knife forward again in a menacing gesture.

These lads had no real beef with the couple; they were doing what they were doing just because they could. They loved the power. It made them feel like they were something.

'How about I slice your fucking ears off?' asked Gold Chain.

He moved the blade forward once more, but suddenly felt an iron grip restrain his wrist.

'What the...?'

His words were cut short as Carter viciously twisted the boy's knife hand, snapping the wrist tendons. The blade fell harmlessly to the ground.

Gold Chain sank to his knees screaming in excruciating pain and looking at his now limp right wrist bent at an impossible angle.

Carter regarded the other two. Both were not quite sure what they had just registered.

Goatee then made a move for something in his pocket. It would be a futile effort. Carter drove the heel of his hand into Goatee's nose and he reeled backwards, blood spurting all over his shirt. He hit the concrete floor of the platform like a stone.

Zit Boy began to flounder. Suddenly, his cocky arrogance was gone. Carter grabbed a handful of his hoodie and pulled him forward to drive a sledgehammer punch into his belly. The air rushed out of his lungs as he dropped to his knees, heaving.

'Now, why don't you little boys fuck off while you can?' Carter said.

His voice was low, but the tone carried real menace.

Gold Chain staggered to his feet and so eventually did Zit Boy, after having deposited the contents of his stomach over the platform floor. They both helped pull Goatee up. His face was a mass of blood and his legs resembled Bambi on ice.

'You prick, we'll have you for this, mark my fucking words!' snarled Gold Chain as he cradled his shattered hand.

They began to back off the platform.

Zit boy rubbed the vomit from his lips with the sleeve of his jacket and shouted, 'You don't realise who you're fucking with, man, and who we work for. None of you losers do. You heard of Lenny Keating?'

'Wasn't he the lead singer in Boyzone?' retorted Carter sarcastically.

Zit boy snorted in disgust.

'Very funny, asshole. Keating is the Governor around here, and you are a fucking dead man.'

'Yeah, fucking dead,' echoed the other two.

The three lads then exited the station platform.

Momentarily, Carter was transported back to that night on the door with the two lads with baseball bats. He should have learnt a lesson from that, but he could not have just sat there and watched the boy and girl get hurt.

He knew that he still had a violent temper. These days, he mostly kept it in check. But when the red mist descended, he found it difficult to control his emotions. Tonight, he had done what he did to help out. He hated bullies.

He looked at the boy and girl.

'Thanks, Mister,' said the boy.

'Yeah, we are really grateful,' agreed the girl.

Carter smiled. 'Forget it. It was nothing.'

'Nothing!' said the boy, 'Jesus, you took those jokers out like John fucking Wick!'

Carter was already walking back to his seat.

The older man with the phone rose from his bench and popped out his earbuds. He nodded in Gary's direction.

'You did a grand job, son. Kids these days have no respect; not like that back in my day.'

The boy turned to his girlfriend.

'That dude is something special. He certainly knows how to look after himself. He was like a freaking ninja.'

They both watched Carter sit back down on his seat with admiration in their eyes.

The announcer on the loudspeaker suddenly spoke: 'The train now coming into the station is the delayed 22:00hrs service to Cardiff.'

Inside the station toilets, the three lads licked their wounds.

Their evening had been a binge of alcohol and coke, and they had felt like the 'Kings of the Castle' until they ran into the stranger on the platform.

'Fuck that bastard. I'm gonna have to go to hospital. I think my wrist is broken,' said Gold Chain.

Goatee was checking his nose in the cracked bathroom mirror.

Zit Boy, though, was animated. He tapped a small amount of white powder from a plastic bag onto the sink top, and snorted it up from a rolled-up twenty-pound note.

'Yesss! Fuck me. That's better,' he shouted. He looked at the other two. 'I tell you what, that dude isn't getting away with this. He can't fuck with us and just walk. I'm going to teach that cunt a lesson. The Ice Squad don't take any shit. He's going to get his.'

'What are you going to do? 'questioned Goatee.

Zit Boy headed for the door. 'Just get ready to fucking run when I come back.'

'Hey, dude. Wait one minute. Don't do anything crazy,' called Gold Chain.

It was too late. The boy had gone.

Carter stood up and grabbed his bag. He was glad to be moving, to get away from here. Time to shape up, soldier, and track this Tony Slade down. He vowed that, once he had done so, he would return to the States and sort his life out. He now felt more positive. He had a mission to complete first. He needed to find his man.

Concentrating on getting onto the incoming train, Carter had not noticed Zit Boy sneak back onto the platform and head towards him. His hoodie was pulled high and tight, obscuring his features from CCTV cameras and the few other commuters. His swagger was back as he walked quickly with purpose.

Carter was standing on the platform's edge, concentrating on the train approaching. He then heard the voices of the boy and girl he had helped earlier shout, 'Look out, Mister!'

But it was too late…

Zit Boy shoved Carter hard in the back, and he toppled off the edge of the platform as the train rode in.

The boy and girl stood frozen in shock.

Carter hit the tracks face-first hard. He was stunned.

The train driver tried in vain to bring the locomotive to a halt in a screech of brakes, but Gary Carter was run over before he could get to his feet.

The girl screamed and buried her face into her boyfriend's shoulder.

Zit Boy ran off laughing, meeting his mates at the station exit.

The three of them disappeared into the night.

Chapter one

Matagorda, Lanzarote, Canary Islands

It was a warm twenty-two degrees on a late February evening. Normally by this time of year, a cool breeze would be blowing across the island in the evenings, bringing a chill to the air. But in the last few weeks, Lanzarote had been having a bit of a mini-heatwave, with temperatures above even their seasonal best.

The bars and restaurants were packed with holiday-makers. Inside and outside, each establishment was busy. The rich smells of different foods being cooked hung in the air. Ice cold beers, wines, and sangria were being ordered like they were going out of fashion.

Ray's Seafront Bar and Grill was a popular haunt for the Brits. It had a typical Canarian design on the outside, but British decor on the inside. This was due to the former owner, who was now deceased.

Ray Steele had been a tough and uncompromising man from North East England who had moved out to Lanzarote in his retirement years and bought this place. If Ray had been your friend, you could wish for no better. If he had been your enemy, then beware.

Ray had lived a violent existence. Coming out to Lanzarote, he hoped he would leave that part of his life behind. And for a while, he did. He married and shared many happy times until his wife sadly passed away from cancer.

He somehow got through those dark days without her, and the pain of loss eased. But, unexpectedly, violence finally caught up with him again, resulting in his untimely death.

The establishment was now managed by Camilo and Lucy Sánchez. They had both managed the place when Ray was alive. They had looked upon him as a father figure and had loved him.

Camilo was born on the island; Lucy was English. She had lived on the Canaries as part of her former employment as a travel rep, and had fallen in love with the place.

Whilst there, she had met Camilo, who was waiting on tables in a hotel where she was stationed with her job. They began dating and fell in love. After a whirlwind romance, they had married, and the rest was history, so to speak.

After Ray's untimely death, they would have loved to have bought the business and kept it running in his honour, but they could not afford the asking price. Ray's last will and testament stipulated that Camilo and Lucy should stay on and work the premises until a suitable buyer came along. He had allocated enough funds for wages and bills for a year.

Most of the money from the sale would go to his late wife Ellen's children. However, he had left his 1967 Ford Thunderbird convertible to Camilo, as he knew that he always loved it. It was still Camilo's prize possession.

When the year was coming to its end and the place had still not sold, Camilo and Lucy started to worry that they would not only lose their jobs, but also their home. Then what could only be described as a miracle happened.

They received a letter from the bank informing them that a mystery benefactor had bought the business and would like them to carry on running the bar and grill. It was business as usual. It was not until a few months ago that they had finally found out who their new boss was.

In Ray's memory, Camilo and Lucy had kept the original name of the business. *Ray's Seafront Bar and Grill* was doing really well, and Camilo and Lucy loved the place.

At first, they missed Ray not being around, but gradually they began to put their own stamp on the business, and it was finally feeling like theirs. The owner was quite happy with this arrangement and remained a sleeping partner.

Matagorda, where the bar was located, was at the quieter end of Puerto Del Carmen. It still had a good atmosphere, with a brilliant selection of bars (Jazz, Irish) and restaurants (Japanese, Chinese, and Spanish), as well as a Spar supermarket.

Matagorda's close location to the airport made it a favourite spot for plane spotters. Its nightlife attracted a high concentration of Irish tourists. Sports enthusiasts also enjoyed Matagorda because of its long promenade, which was ideal for runners, cyclists, and those just wanting to take a stroll. The promenade connected right through to Puerto del Carmen in one direction and Playa Honda and the capital Arrecife in the other direction. Matagorda's beach was popular with windsurfers, too, and had been awarded blue flag status in 2009.

Camilo and Lucy loved Matagorda and were happy and proud to call it home. They enjoyed being part of such a vibrant and exciting holiday resort scene. They were determined now, with the unexpected injection of money, to make a success of the business.

And they needed to. A few days ago, they had found out that they were going to be parents. Lucy was two months pregnant with their first child. Life could not be better for them at present.

In the cool dark interior of the bar, a man sat quietly at a corner table. An overhead fan blew a gentle breeze down from above. He sipped whiskey on the rocks and listened to the live entertainment on a small stage at the far end of the restaurant.

Tonight, it was Molly – a young and talented Irish female singer and guitarist. She played every Friday and Saturday at Ray's and was extremely popular.

At present, she was halfway through a brilliant acoustic version of *Whiskey in the Jar* by Thin Lizzy.

The bar and grill was pretty much packed with couples and families. The resort of Matagorda was a great place for people who just wanted to chill and unwind.

The man glanced towards the bar, caught Camilo and Lucy's attention, and raised his glass in acknowledgement. He was feeling in a mellow mood. Maybe it was the whiskey or maybe, for once in a long time, he was feeling relaxed.

His journey to this point in his life could only be described as remarkable for many reasons. At this moment, he was simply happy to be alive and to be soaking up this infectious ambience.

Suddenly, the laid-back atmosphere was disturbed by the sound of breaking glass.

The man's senses clicked to red alert; he could sense trouble. A bubble of adrenaline popped in his belly. He scanned the area, looking for the source of the noise. He quickly noticed that it had been a youngster with his family who had knocked his glass of cola off the table.

One of the waiters on duty, a young man named Diego, came over and efficiently sorted out the situation with the minimum of fuss. Everything returned to normal.

The man finished his drink, got up from the table, and walked out onto the street. Warmth glowed in the darkness from other restaurants, bars, and shops, along this busy strip. He looked across the road to the beach and the sea. A few lights from fishing boats twinkled in the inky blackness. He could hear the waves crashing onto the shore.

He was about to return inside when raised voices caught his attention. Walking along the esplanade and getting closer were two men and a woman. The woman was remonstrating with both men about something. Both the men responded aggressively towards her.

The man kept a close eye on them as they drew level with the bar and grill. They seemed to have had a few too many drinks and were arguing. The man appraised them.

Both men were, he estimated, in their late forties. Both were solidly built, but the muscle they'd had in their younger years had now turned to flab. They sported faded tattoos on their arms underneath lobster pink suntans. The woman was a little younger. She was slim and attractive with dark hair and a dark tan.

He listened to the conversation as they were now in earshot. The men were British. They were insisting that she have another drink with them, but the woman was telling them that she was going back to her hotel. She spoke good English but with a Spanish accent. As she went to walk away, one of the men grabbed her arm.

The man stepped forward. 'Is there some problem here?'

Both men turned in his direction. The one with the shaven head, the biggest of the two, regarded him.

'There is no problem, pal, so mind your own business and piss off.'

The man had heard these sorts of comments many times before. It was like water off a duck's back to him.

'Well, I think the lady wants to go, so I suggest you take your hands off her and let her go on her way.'

The other man, who wore a baseball cap and sported a trendy long beard, now joined in.

'Or what, pal?'

The man remained calm, but the situation was now drawing an audience.

If both of these clowns had not been so full of alcohol and cocky bravado, they would have looked into this man's eyes and seen something there – something that you did not want to provoke. But they were too drunk and too stupid to do so.

'Beardy' stepped up closer to the man, and his mate followed suit.

'I asked you, or what? What the fuck are you going to do?'

The man subtly shifted his body weight as he stepped back. Both these jokers should have seen it, but they were amateurs. The man facing them was not. He had been here hundreds of times in the past. He looked into their glazed eyes. They were not a threat to him.

'I am going to ask you one more time. Let her go and be on your way. It isn't worth it.'

Both men sneered.

'Fuck you, asshole. How about you piss off and mind your own business or I'll give you a slap for your trouble?' said 'Baldy', who was shaping up to throw a sucker punch.

The man could see it a mile away. As he suspected, they were amateurs.

As they both made their move forward, the man jabbed the 'V' of his open lead hand into Baldy's windpipe, and at the same time back-hand slapped Beardy in the balls. They were both pulled up abruptly by the speed of the sudden attack and immediately incapacitated.

Any fight in them had gone, along with their bravado.

The man stared hard at both of them. When he spoke, his voice was low and controlled, but carried a chilling menace.

'We are done here. Don't push it, or I promise you this, if you don't fuck off, I am really going to be forced to hurt you both badly.'

There was a moment of hesitation on the faces of both men. There was also fear in their eyes. Now it was as if they were looking at this man for the first time and they could sense danger.

The man continued staring, and without taking his eyes off them, he called back over his shoulder to Camilo who had stopped what he was doing at the bar and was watching the scenario unfolding.

'Camilo, you better phone for an ambulance to come immediately. I think we may need it.'

Both men regarded each other. The man knew they were done.

'Do the right thing. Go home and sleep it off. Leave the girl be.'

Both men seemed rooted to the spot, and for a second, it looked like they were going to make a move forward again, but then they decided otherwise. Their fight and their bottle had gone, like bath water down a plug hole.

They began to walk away.

When they were at a safe distance, Beardy, who had regained a little of his swagger, shouted,

'This isn't fucking over, pal. Believe me.'

The man walked forward. He now had to turn the screw and make sure these boys did not come back later looking for revenge.

'Yes, it fucking is. I am here now waiting if you want to try your luck. Why walk away? Let's fucking do it now, mano to mano, and finish it. But I promise you, I will fucking crush you both.'

Both men regarded him; their talk had all been bluff in an attempt to save face. They snuck off into the night, muttering threats under their breath, with their tails between their legs.

The man watched them go.

'Camilo, cancel that ambulance. We are all good.'

Camilo smiled and shouted back, 'Yes, boss.'

The man felt his adrenaline begin to subside and he took a deep breath.

The woman came towards him.

'Thank you for what you done. I am grateful. They were pestering me in a bar further down the road, and when I left, they followed me. I couldn't get rid of them.'

The man turned and faced her. He smiled.

'No worries. They've gone now. Go into the bar and get a drink on the house. When you're ready to leave, I'll order you a taxi.'

The woman nodded. 'Thank you. That is kind of you.'

She extended a slim hand. 'By the way, my name is Gabriela García.'

The man shook her offered hand.

'Pleased to meet you, Gabriela. I am Tony. Tony Sla... I mean, Swan. I am the owner of this place.'

Chapter two

Tony Slade woke up to the morning sun shining through a gap in the bedroom curtains. His left leg was burning hot from where the rays shone onto his exposed limb hanging out of the sheets.

He rolled to the opposite side of the bed, away from the sunlight, to let himself wake up fully and focus on the day. Finally, he turned over to look at the bedside clock. It read 7:30am.

He threw back the covers, got out of bed, and stretched his arms high above his head. He regarded himself in the wardrobe mirror.

These days, he sported a short, well-groomed beard. It matched his short salt and pepper hair. Distinguished might be the term to describe his appearance.

He was still in decent enough shape for a man not far short of his sixtieth birthday. He worked out daily – an old habit he still kept from his military career. The Mediterranean sun over the past month had also given him a nice tan.

He could still make out the faint scars of the three bullet wounds that could have claimed his life a few years back. He had been lucky, although it had not felt that way at the time.

Tony went into the bathroom, turned on the shower faucet and got it to the temperature he liked, then he stepped in and closed the curtain.

The water felt good on his body. He shampooed his hair and then applied shower gel all over. When he stepped out of the shower ten minutes later, he felt revitalised and alive.

He headed for the kitchen to brew some coffee. Black and strong. He liked his coffee. As he waited for the coffee to drip through the percolator, he looked out of the upstairs window of his flat which was located above the restaurant.

The morning sun reflected off the blue ocean across the road. A few locals were already out on the rocks fishing. A sprinkling of people were also out walking, jogging, or cycling along the seafront, getting their exercise in before the sun rose too high in the sky.

He thought back to the previous evening and the encounter with the two aggressive men. When he had helped lock up the restaurant at the end of the night with Camilo, he had kept vigilant just in case the pair of jokers had fancied coming back, but all had been quiet. As he had deduced earlier, they were a pair of paper tigers. Bullies.

He also thought about the drink he had shared with the woman Gabriela. It had been nice. It was the first drink he had shared with a woman alone since Annette.

Tony felt a pang of sorrow inside when he thought of the only woman that he had genuinely loved in such an awfully long time, and how she had been violently and cruelly taken away from him. A beautiful life snuffed out in a moment of madness and violence. It still hurt him. But now, instead of a raw pain, it was a dull ache.

The drink with Gabriela had been nothing really. Just playing the good Samaritan, but all the same it had felt strange. Maybe he was finally ready to move on with his life.

His military career had provided no time for any serious relationships. Just now and again, a casual one-night stand.

Apart from Annette, there had only been one other girl he thought he might have shared a life with, but he had been a naive teenager back then, and he had blown that relationship.

Thinking back to the previous evening, he still had to be careful not to reveal his true identity. He had to remember he was Tony Swan for now, not Tony Slade.

Tony was enjoying the sunshine of Lanzarote and the laid-back lifestyle. He was feeling fit and healthy and seemed to have got his self in a good place after all the recent drama of his time on the island Graig O Mor.

He thought back to the incident with killer Andy Roth, DCI John Wyatt, the police, and his chance rescue from the cold Bristol Channel by Joe Walsh and Danny Ewan, when he felt certain his time had well and truly come.

When he had been picked up in the helicopter from the sea, his joy was short-lived, as he thought the men who had saved him from a watery grave were going to put him back in it. But, in a strange twist of fate, that was not to be.

He was flown back to Newcastle – his home city – and released safely. Walsh and Ewan were good to their word about this. The only stipulation was that he moved on by the end of the week, as there were a few people not so forgiving in the city over his involvement with the death of local villain Kenny Robbins.

He had holed up in a hotel, sleeping most of the time and eating good food to build his strength. He'd kept a low profile, and by Sunday, using the fake ID and passport under the name of Tony Swan, he had flown out of Newcastle International to Morocco and its capital Rabat. He needed to be somewhere safe to have some time to think.

He had planned to come to Morocco with Annette when they were going to run away together, and had looked into the logistics of it. Sadly, it had never materialised. Annette and many others had tragically lost their lives in what had now become known as the infamous 'Coffee Shop Massacre'.

Tony had a contact in Morocco, though; another ex-army buddy, Brian James.

Brian had also been a good friend of Ray Steele.

Ray had been Tony's mentor and close friend back in his early days working the doors in the North East. He had taught him the Japanese art of Jujutsu, and how to survive on some of the toughest club doors.

Brian James had also trained under Ray's tutelage. At Tony's request, Brian travelled the hundred odd miles from the north coast of Africa down to Matagorda in Lanzarote and covertly found out the business situation with Ray's bar and grill. Brian informed him that the business would go under if the management did not find a new backer.

Tony knew Camilo and Lucy who ran the place. He had met them a few years back when he had visited Ray, and he liked them both. With £250,000 of villain Kenny Robbins' money burning a hole in his pocket, Tony made the investment with the help of a bank manager and solicitor who were not too worried about the fact that he was going to pay in cold hard cash or where it had come from, as long as they got their cut.

He had not contacted Camilo or Lucy Instead, he had just turned up out of the blue some weeks back once the deal was signed and sealed, and revealed that he was their new boss and 'sleeping' partner. They were both thrilled to see Tony and over the moon with the business arrangements.

Camilo and Lucy knew Tony's real identity and his past. They also knew Ray Steele had thought of him as a son, and they had no problem with keeping his real identity a secret. So, with the future of the bar and grill settled, Tony decided to stay in Lanzarote for a while.

It was a blessing at present, because Brexit still had not been settled, so UK citizens could stay in Lanzarote without the need for a visa. This certainly suited Tony's present needs, and he was happy with the arrangement.

He had lost so many people near to him in the last few years that he was personally still in a bit of a daze. He had no idea what he was going to do next.

Tony realised that the police in the UK would leave the file open on him, especially after the murder of DCI Wyatt, even though he'd had nothing directly to do with it.

Spain and its accompanying islands were no longer the safe haven for UK criminals as they had been in the 1970s and 1980s. New extradition treaties had seen to that.

Tony had limited time here before, once more, he would have to move on again.

For most of his life he had travelled from pillar to post in the army, and there was nowhere that he could truly call home.

He had heard through the grapevine that Sergeant Steve Richmond – DCI Wyatt's right-hand man – had made a full recovery from his fall from the cliff on Graig O Mor island, and was back at work. Word had it that he was still determined to find Tony to avenge the death of his boss.

At the moment, Lanzarote would do, and by being here he felt close to his old friend Ray, and he liked that. He owed the man so much. He had given his life to help Tony. Buying the business and keeping Ray's name going in some small way helped repay his friend's ultimate sacrifice.

He took his coffee and walked down into the restaurant. It had a smattering of early morning customers for breakfast. Tony sat down at an outside table and breathed in the warm morning air, then looked across the road to the beautiful vista of the sea.

After six months on the cold barren island of Graig O Mor in the grey waters of the Bristol Channel, this was truly paradise. A paradise that he'd thought at one time he would never see again. Tony Slade seemed to have more lives than a cat, but recently he had come remarkably close to using up the last one.

He was interrupted from his thoughts by the voice of Camilo calling from inside the restaurant. 'Morning, boss. Can I get you some breakfast?'

Tony acknowledged his friend.

'Morning, Camilo. No thanks, I have all I need right here, thank you.' He raised his coffee cup in a salute.

Camilo waved back.

'Okay. Maybe a refill in a little while, yes?'

Tony nodded his agreement.

Suddenly, a shadow covered the table and Tony looked up to see two men looming over him. It was the two men that he'd had trouble with the previous evening. Tony's hand tightened on the cup of hot coffee, ready to throw it in their direction if something kicked off.

'What the fuck do you two want?' he asked aggressively.

The two men regarded Tony warily. They both looked worse for wear, and neither had the bravado they had displayed last night.

Then the bearded one spoke.

'Look, mate, we aren't here for trouble. We came back to apologise and say we're sorry.'

The bald one now chimed in, 'We had too much sun and too much beer yesterday. We acted like a pair of pricks. We have come in this place a few times and like it. We wanted to clear the air and hoped that we would be welcome in here again.'

Tony could not believe his ears. This did not happen very often. Especially in his life.

He relaxed somewhat and looked at the men. He had been in enough violent situations to sense these guys were genuine. He stood up from the table, and both men took an uneasy step back.

'Okay, guys. Apologies accepted. It took a lot of balls to come back here and do this. I respect you for that. So, we are all good.'

He extended his hand, which both men readily shook.

'May we come in for breakfast?' asked Beardy.

Tony sat back down. 'Sure. Why not?'

Both men nodded and walked into the restaurant.

Tony watched them go and nodded to Camilo who had been watching in the background that everything was cool.

He went back to his coffee.

Well, well, well. Miracles can happen now and again. *This just might turn out to be a good day*, he mused.

Chapter three

Detective Inspector Steve Richmond sat at his cluttered desk, sipping on a mug of dark brown sludge masquerading as coffee. It was another Monday morning in Bridewell Police Station, CID division, Bristol.

Outside, the rain came down from a slate grey sky. It did not brighten Richmond's mood. His stomach growled with hunger. He could murder a bacon sandwich right now, but Marie, his on/off partner of five years, had him on the 5:2 diet.

This fad diet had you eat normally for five days and then fast for two. The fasting days drastically reduced your calorie intake, ensuring some weight loss.

Richmond was not a fan, but after being out of work on sick leave and being pretty much immobilised for a few months, he had piled on some unwanted pounds.

Marie was a regular gym bunny and ate healthily, so she was determined to get Richmond into the same lifestyle. She knew she would have an uphill struggle on her hands when, on his previous fast day, she had caught Richmond in the garden shed swallowing down a Mars bar and a grab-bag of salt and vinegar McCoy's crisps as if they were going out of fashion.

Bollocks to it, thought Richmond.

He shouted out of his open office door for Sergeant Luke Drury.

Presently, a head popped around the door frame.

'You called, Gov?'

'Yeah, Luke. Are you going out for any brekkie this morning?'

Luke Drury's face broke into a grin.

He was a good-looking, blond-haired young man, twenty-six years of age, and Oxford educated. He was a clever detective and Richmond liked him.

Drury had been assigned to work with him since he came back to work some six weeks ago, and they seemed to hit it off straight away. The younger man was ambitious and definitely on the ladder upwards to bigger and better things.

He had a wise head on young shoulders. Married, and had a two-year-old toddler. His wife of three years, Tessa, was a real looker. Ex-model apparently. The perfect couple. Luke Drury was certainly a solid candidate for promotion down the line.

Steve Richmond had got his own recent promotion to Inspector. It had been a poignant moment when he'd received it, as it was his former boss DCI John Wyatt who had pushed him to go for it.

Richmond would have loved him to have been there when the news was announced. Wyatt, however, had tragically lost his life in the incident on the island of Graig O Mor.

Wyatt had been an excellent policeman, a good friend, and mentor. Richmond missed him every day and often expected him to walk into the office at any time and throw his trademark grey overcoat over the back of the chair and ask, 'What have we got on today, Steve?'

Richmond was determined to follow in his late boss's footsteps and be a good copper. No matter what had happened at the end of Wyatt's life, he'd had a solid arrest record and had been one of the best. He was missed by all.

Richmond could have lost his own life in the same incident, when he fell down a cliff. He had been lucky. A concussion, a fractured left leg, and two broken ribs, were the injuries he had sustained as a result of the fall. It had kept him off work for five months.

'Want me to bring you something back? What do you need? Yoghurt? Cereal bar? Banana?'

Everybody in CID seemed to know about Richmond's diet.

'Very funny, pal. I want a bacon sarnie with plenty of ketchup. I am fucking starving.'

Richmond handed Drury a £5-note. 'I expect to see some change as well.'

Drury took the money.

'Should I just run this by the lovely Marie first, Gov?'

Richmond threw an empty file in the young sergeant's direction.

'Fuck off before I bust your ass back to traffic.'

Drury backed out of the office holding his hands up in mock surrender. 'Okay, I'm going.'

Richmond went back to studying the notes on one of his latest cases – another gang-related stabbing. A young black lad by the name of Leon Joseph had been knifed to death in a local park. No CCTV footage and no witnesses, or at least nobody was owning up to having seen what had happened.

Leon had been fourteen years of age. What a fucking waste of life. Early indicators pointed towards drug involvement.

Back in the days when Richmond was a teenager, you settled disputes with a straightener – a fist fight. When it was done, it was done. Most of the time you both shook hands and it was forgotten. Where the fuck did it all go wrong?

The UK crime scene was getting more like the States every day. Gangs and drugs seemed to be everywhere, and the suspects were getting younger. When you shut one operation down, another appeared. It was like sticking your finger in a leaking dam.

His trail of thought was interrupted by a knock on his open office door. Richmond looked up to see PC Debbie Garrett standing holding a manilla file.

'Hello, Gov. Thought you might want to check this out.'

'Come in, Garrett. What have you got?'

PC Garrett walked in and placed the file on her boss's desk.

Richmond knew her as a good solid copper. Smart, but also a tough cookie, despite the blonde locks and model good looks. She was also a seasoned black belt in some sort of 'Hong Kong Phooey' art, and liked a scrap.

'A body on the railway lines at Temple Meads Station. Found late Saturday night,' she said.

Richmond picked up the file.

'Suicide? Murder?'

'It seems he was pushed.'

'Witnesses?'

'Yes, a young couple who were on the platform when it happened.'

'Do we know who the victim was?' asked Richmond.

Garrett flipped open the file.

'Yes, Gov. The dead man's name was Gary Carter, an American ex-Marine. His passport states he still lives in New York. It was stamped for a month in the UK. Apparently, he helped this couple out of a spot of bother with a gang of youths. Allegedly, one of them returned for payback, and pushed him onto the tracks.'

Just like the fucking States, mused Richmond.

He reached out and picked up the file.

'Okay, Garrett. So, what am I looking for here? I take it the couple gave a statement and we are pursuing CCTV footage?'

Garrett nodded. 'Yes, Gov. That's all in hand.'

Richmond dropped the file back on the desk. His empty belly growled again.

Garrett continued, 'I attended this incident with DCI Bob Pritchard, but he was called off the case last night as his wife has gone into labour. Chief Superintendent Hardwick apparently asked for you to be assigned to it.'

'Did he, now? I am honoured. Good old Hard Dick, always handy at passing the buck.'

Richmond and his former Governor DCI Wyatt had pissed off Hardwick over the Graig O Mor case. They had kept the Chief Super out of the loop, and he had not been happy about it. Maybe this was his way of payback. Since returning to work, Richmond had enjoyed an uneasy truce with his superior.

'So, spit it out, Garrett. What do you think is of interest here for me?'

'It was something that was found in his jacket pocket. It was a newspaper clipping.'

'Come on then. The suspense is fucking killing me.'

Richmond reached for his coffee cup and took a gulp. It did not taste any better cold.

Garrett continued, 'The newspaper clipping was about an old friend of yours. Tony Slade.'

Steve Richmond nearly choked on his drink.

Tony Slade. Well, there was a name that he had not heard for a while. But he had not forgotten him. The bastard was indirectly responsible for his Governor's death.

'Any ideas what this Carter guy was up to over here?'

Garrett shook her head. 'Not as yet.'

Richmond reopened the file.

'Thanks, Garrett. When Sergeant Drury returns, accompany him to check on the CCTV footage from the station for me, will you?'

Garrett seemed pleased to be involved.

'Right, Gov. I'm on it.' She turned and left the room.

Richmond flicked through the file.

Another brutal and unnecessary death in Bristol. That on its own was a choker. But the burning question in his mind right now was what this dead ex-American soldier was doing with a newspaper clipping of Tony Slade in his pocket at a Bristol train station?

Chapter four

Ruby Carter gazed out of the large glass window of her office inside the *Manhattan News* building in downtown Brooklyn. She looked directly across at the iconic architecture of the famous Williamsburgh Savings Bank Tower skyscraper. No matter how many times she looked at the tower, it never failed to impress her.

At present, New York was experiencing snowfall, but the whole surrounding area was still buzzing with people going about their business.

Since the rezoning of Downtown Brooklyn in 2004, the area had been undergoing a transformation, with $9 billion of private investment and $300 million in public improvements underway. The area was becoming a hub for education. In 2017, New York University had announced that it would invest over $500 million to renovate and expand the NYU Tandon School of Engineering and its surrounding Downtown Brooklyn-based campus.

Ruby loved being right in the heart of things, and she enjoyed her job as a line editor for her late father's business. At the minute, everything concerning the business was up in the air and in the hands of the lawyers. For now, she found herself with the daunting task of being in charge of the whole company.

She was thankful for the help and experience of Freddie Golding, a senior executive and trusted friend of Clint Carter, in the business.

She wanted to do a good job and also make a good impression on all her staff and employees, but part of her mind was on her brother Gary and whether he had any news for her.

She moved away from the window. Picking up her phone from the desktop, she checked it for the umpteenth time for any messages from her brother. There were none. She dropped it back down again in frustration. She had not heard anything from Gary for a few days.

He had promised to keep her updated every evening about his visit to England, and had done so up until last Saturday. Since then, there had been nothing, and he was not answering his phone either. She could not help but feel worried.

Sure, Gary could look after himself, but all the same, he was her brother and, although only briefly, they had recently reconnected again after their father's passing.

He had been only too willing to go to England and track down this man Tony Slade. Ruby knew it would not be easy. Maybe Tony Slade was dead? Maybe he was in another country? Maybe he had changed his name?

After all, he was ex-military, which meant he would know how to hide his tracks, but then again, so was her brother and she knew he would do his best.

But in recent years, he himself had gone off the radar, and had been drinking heavily and just about scrapping a living. He was a long time out of the Marines, and certainly not the man he used to be.

Ruby had the first flicker of doubt about whether her brother was up to her request. Maybe she had pushed him too hard to help? Maybe she should have left the past in the past?

She checked her phone one more time and then put it in her pocket. She was due a lunch meeting with Freddie at *Joey's Burrito Stop* across the block, and she was running late.

....

When Ruby returned to her apartment that evening, she still had not heard anything. She dialled Gary's number, but it rang and rang and then went to voicemail. She left a message and hung up.

As she made her way towards the bathroom to run a bath, she could not shake off the feeling of unease that she had sensed all day. She hoped a long soak might soothe away some of the tension.

DI Steve Richmond stood in the city morgue, looking at the remains of Gary Carter. For a moment, he thought he might see the bacon sandwich he had eaten earlier making a reappearance.

'Fuck me. What a mess,' he muttered.

The body had been effectively torn in half at the torso.

'That's what happens when you get hit by a train. Even if it was slowing down.'

Richmond regarded the man standing next to him. Terry Hutchins was the forensic pathologist assigned to this case. He was a bear of a man, and quite an intimidating looking character with his bushy grey beard and piercing green eyes.

They had worked together many times in the past and Richmond knew that, in Hutchins' case, appearances could be deceiving.

Hutchins had been married to his wife Mary for thirty-five years and was a doting grandfather of four. Terry was a gentle giant. He also knew his job.

'Seen enough, Steve?' Hutchins asked.

Richmond nodded and walked away towards the door.

'Fancy a coffee, Terry? I'm paying.'

The big man pulled the cover back over the body on the steel trolley, slid it back into refrigeration, and shut the door.

'Sure. Give me a minute.'

He pulled off a pair of surgical gloves and deposited them into a waste bin, then washed his hands methodically and dried them. He slipped off his gown and grabbed a sports jacket from a peg on the back of the door and shrugged it on. 'OK, ready'.

The two men stood by the coffee machine. Richmond was feeding coins into it.

'So, Terry, anything of note with the body?'

Terry ran his hand through his beard and shook his head.

'No, Steve. It was just a routine autopsy. Obviously, cause of death was collision with the train and the resulting trauma. He literally wouldn't have had time to know what hit him before death.'

Richmond handed Hutchins his coffee.

'Time of death ties up with the witness statements.'

The big man nodded. 'Yep. Around 22:30.'

'Are the victim's clothes here or with the crime lab technicians?' asked Richmond.

Hutchins took a sip of his coffee.

'Clothes and personal belongings went to the crime lab up on the second floor. I believe Harriet Grey is dealing with them. There wasn't much.'

'Okay. Thanks, Terry. I'll go and check them out.'

They finished their coffee over small talk, then both men shook hands.

'Good to see you on the mend, Steve. I also wanted to extend my condolences about your Governor. He was one of the best.' said Hutchins.

Richmond nodded his acknowledgement and headed for the exit.

Once outside, he breathed in the fresh air. No matter how many times he went in that place, it took a while to get the cloying smell of death out of his nostrils.

He walked across a small expanse of neatly mown grass, which led him into another part of the building, got into a lift and hit the button for the second floor.

'Hello, Harriet. How is that waster of a husband of yours?'

'Hello, Steve. He's fine. How's the diet going, fat boy?' replied Harriet Grey.

They both laughed and embraced.

Harriet Grey was the chief technician of the lab and had been working for the police for twenty years. She was an attractive brunette in her early fifties. Her husband Larry had been a policeman in the force here in

Bristol before retiring last year. Richmond knew both of them well, professionally and socially. Harriet cooked a mean spaghetti bolognese and made an explosive margarita.

Richmond was now standing in the crime tech lab. It was a big, brightly lit room with about half a dozen technicians in white lab coats crouched over tables, busily engrossed in their work.

'So, to what do I owe this pleasure?' she asked.

'I'm assigned to the Gary Carter case. The American.'

Harriet nodded. 'Ah, the train victim. Right. How can I help you, Steve?'

'I would like to see his belongings, if that's possible?'

'Yes, of course. Follow me.'

Harriet got up from her desk and walked towards a long bench at the far end of the room. Richmond followed and could not help glance at the sexy sway of Harriet's hips as she walked ahead. Damn, Larry was a lucky old bastard.

'Here we go, Steve. There isn't a lot, but it's all laid out here.'

Richmond regarded the tabletop.

On it was an empty battered green holdall. Next to it were its contents. There were a few t-shirts – one black with an AC/DC logo on it, and one white with the words 'Semper Fidelis'.

'What's that mean?' Richmond asked.

Harriet smiled. 'I took time to look it up on the web. It is the US Marine Corps motto. It means "always faithful".'

'Very good, Harriet. Not just a pretty face then,' joked Richmond.

He moved along to inspect a plain grey sweatshirt, underwear, and socks.

Next was a passport, which Richmond picked up after slipping on a pair of latex gloves offered by Harriet. First, he studied the photograph of Carter. The man stared confidently into the camera lens. He looked like a man who could handle himself.

The passport was stamped with a few US internal flights to Boston, Washington DC, Pittsburgh, and Baltimore, before the British flight.

There were also two dog-eared paperback books. One was *The Late Show* by Michael Connelly. Richmond had read a fair few of Connelly's novels; he liked them. The other was the famous autobiographical account of T.E. Lawrence's (aka Lawrence of Arabia) time in World War One, called *The Seven Pillars of Wisdom*.

There was also an empty packet of Marlboro cigarettes, a cheap plastic zippo lighter, a Mars bar, and a packet of spearmint chewing gum. He also found a copy of *The Sun* newspaper that was nearly a week old, and next to that, a small black Maglite torch and a 4-inch folding pen knife, with a carved wooden handle with the profile of a wolf on it.

Richmond then saw a plastic file which seemed to be full of photocopied papers. On opening the file, he was immediately interested in the contents. They were all copies of newspaper articles referring to Tony Slade and the 'Coffee Shop Massacre' here in Bristol.

This is how Richmond himself had first encountered Slade, when the man was admitted to hospital after being shot. Richmond had taken an instant dislike to him. He thought that he was too cocky and also that he was hiding something. When Slade did a runner from the hospital and disappeared, it only fuelled Richmond's suspicions.

It all came to a head sometime later, on the remote island of Graig O Mor in the Bristol Channel, with violent and tragic consequences. Slade had then disappeared once more. Although the case was still open, the trail had gone cold.

Richmond moved on to survey the bloodstained and ragged remnants of the clothes that the victim had been wearing.

There, next to them, was the newspaper clipping, somehow free of blood or damage. Richmond carefully unfolded it. There was a grainy photograph of Slade in his army uniform. It looked like this guy was tracking Slade down, but why?

'That was everything. As I said, this man travelled light,' remarked Harriet Grey.

Richmond scanned the table again.

'Mobile phone?' he asked.

'It was badly shattered, but we have a technician working on it to see if they can save any information.'

'Let me know if they do as soon as you can, okay?'

Harriet smiled. 'Will do.'

'Thanks, Harriet. I appreciate that.'

They said their goodbyes and Richmond left the building. He walked to his car and jumped in. He started up the Volvo V70 and headed back to the station. As he did so, he used his hands-free mobile set to call Sergeant Luke Drury.

'Yes, Gov?' answered Drury.

'Luke, meet me outside the front of the station in twenty minutes. We need to go and have a chat with a few witnesses from this Carter murder.'

'Righto. I'll be waiting. Listen, Gov. Chief Superintendent Hardwick was looking for you. The press has been hounding him for information on the case. He wants to speak with you asap.'

'Alright. Thanks, Luke. I will deal with that later.'

Richmond hung up the call. He suspected old Hard Dick would be going up the wall. Fuck it, let him sweat.

He was determined to find out what the dead man Carter had been up to and why he was looking for Tony Slade. But he also had to remind himself that this was a murder case, and they needed to find the individual(s) who had pushed Gary Carter to his death.

Slade had never been far from Richmond's thoughts, especially whilst he was recuperating from his injuries.

He had last seen Slade being miraculously airlifted out of the freezing waters of the Bristol Channel by a helicopter. Who was in it was unknown, but he did know that somebody in the helicopter had fired shots from a semi-automatic machine gun towards the beach, which resulted in DCI John Wyatt's death?

The helicopter had disappeared and had never been traced. Richmond suspected some inside help from the harbour police, but could not prove anything. One minute they had Slade there in their grip; the next moment, he had been whisked away to safety.

Since then, there had been no word of him. Once more, the elusive bastard had disappeared.

Although Slade had not pulled the trigger of the gun that had ended his Governor's life, Richmond still held him personally responsible. If there was a remote chance of finding Slade, he was going to take it, and fuck anybody who tried to get in his way. That included Chief Superintendent Timothy 'Hard Dick' Hardwick.

This man Gary Carter might somehow have held a clue to Slade's whereabouts, and Richmond was going to find out their connection. Over the years that they worked together, DCI Wyatt had drummed into him that a good cop would never give up on a case. Those words and ethics ultimately proved the man's own downfall. Richmond was determined not to make the same mistake.

Chapter five

Tony Slade jogged along the seafront. The sun hung low in the evening sky. He enjoyed running at this time. It was 7:15pm and the beach crowds had gone back to their hotels or villas to prepare for their evening dinner, so things were a lot quieter.

He now joined the cycle path on the promenade which ran alongside the seafront towards the airport, and headed on into the town of Playa Honda. The route from Matagorda to Playa Honda afforded some beautiful views of the Atlantic Ocean.

Tony's early evening jogs helped him relax and meditate on his life. Running had been a staple part of his exercise since his army days, and although he couldn't run as fast or freely as he would like, partly due to age and partly due to a few niggling injuries, he still loved it.

He was grateful that he could still enjoy this pleasure, especially after recently recovering from three gunshot wounds – one of which had clipped his lungs.

He tried to put those thoughts from his mind as he ran on.

A few runners coming the other way acknowledged him. They looked like serious athletes.

Every year the resort hosted an Ironman Triathlon in May. Back in his early army days, Tony had participated in one of these gruelling events. He had been part of a small paratrooper team that had competed for a cancer charity after three of the team's member had lost parents to the disease.

The event had taken place in the picturesque seaside town of Youghal in County Cork, Republic of Ireland – a well-known Ironman location.

Tony and the team completed the 2.4-mile swim, 112-mile bicycle ride, and 26.22 mile run in just under twelve hours, which was well below the average estimated time. The fastest recorded time until then had been seven hours, forty minutes, and twenty-three seconds – an incredible achievement set in Brazil by Tim Don of the UK.

It was an unbelievably tough event, even for the high levels of fitness soldiers were expected to have. Tony had been in his twenties then.

As the runners now passed by, he did not envy the task they were training for.

Tony reached the outskirts of Playa Honda – his 2.3-mile mark. He briefly stopped and took in some water before turning around to continue his run back home.

It would roughly be an all-round 5-mile run; not bad for a man knocking on sixty.

Having said that, he remembered a few years back visiting his old mentor Ray Steele out here, and the tough old bastard had run the route with him and he was in his early eighties.

Tony once again felt a pang of sadness for his friend. He still felt a deep loss for a man whom he was honoured to have called a friend and teacher.

Ray Steele had been a legend in his home city of Durham. He had been a master of Japanese Jujutsu and Judo, and had ended his impressive career as a 7th Dan black belt – a high accolade indeed. Ray had also been a veteran of hundreds of altercations when working on the doors of some of the roughest and toughest clubs and pubs in the North East.

Tony had starting learning Jujutsu from Ray as a young boy at the then legendary *Top Dog* gym in Durham, and had gone on to work on the doors with him for a few years before joining the parachute regiment. He had learnt so much from the man, and had marvelled at his coolness and composure when dealing with violence.

One incident that stuck in his mind was one he had witnessed first-hand and which had gone down in North East folklore.

As he ran, he went back in his mind to that place in time.

Ray and Tony had been working on the door of a club named *BB's*. It was a club that drew in a celebrity crowd from all walks of life. On this particular evening, a man and a few of his mates turned up at the club door. They had certainly had a few too many and were in a boisterous mood.

Ray stepped up as head doorman and refused them entry. The man got belligerent and started to posture in front of Ray. He was a big guy, and the broken nose and cauliflower ears suggested he was no stranger to a fight.

'Do you know who the fuck I am, pal?'

Ray remained calm in front of this show of aggression.

'I don't care who you are. You aren't coming in tonight, son.'

The man sneered and looked around at his mates in disbelief.

'Here, lads. Tell this muppet who I am.'

One of the men spoke up immediately.

'This is Barry Fellows. You know, the England rugby international.'

Ray stared at him impassively.

'Never heard of him. Wrong shape ball for me.'

The group of men looked incredulously at each other.

The man spoke again.

'Everybody knows who Barry Fellows is, even a dumb Geordie like you. England and Wigan scrumhalf. Thirty-five caps for his country. Stars in the Shredded Wheat ads on television.'

'Well, I'm not bothered who he is. You guys have had too much to drink and you are not coming in.'

Fellows stepped forward a little.

'How about I see the manager Clive?'

Ray kept arm's length distance and subtly shifted his weight.

'I am the head doorman here, and Clive Robson pays me to decide who is coming in and out. As I said, you aren't coming in. So, why don't you boys head off elsewhere.'

It was obvious Fellows was not used to this type of treatment and neither were his pals.

Fellow's face darkened. 'How about we walk straight in, you cunt?'

You could now cut the atmosphere with a knife.

Ray stared the men down.

'Well, you could always try, but I wouldn't advise it.'

Suddenly, two of the men made a move to push past Ray.

Ray's hands were a blur. A reverse edge of the hand chopped to the neck put one man on his ass, while a sledgehammer headbutt put the other out cold. A third man received a front kick in the stomach, which would have dropped a mule, and he joined his mates in an ungainly tangle of bodies on the ground.

Barry Fellows now hesitated as he saw his pals get lit up in a matter of seconds. Ray stood back now in a fighting stance. Tony and another doorman, Eddie, stood by his side.

'Right, son. Now if you are the big sportsman you say you are, I would think having your kneecap shattered or your arm broken wouldn't go down too well with the rugby bigwigs. But if you step any closer to me, that is exactly what is going to happen to you. Do you really think I would be stood here as head doorman if I couldn't back up my negotiating skills with some fucking hardcore moves? Please don't underestimate me, lad.'

Fellows swallowed hard and then raised his hands.

'I'm going. I've had too much to drink and was out of order. We're done here.'

He stepped back and began to help his mates to their feet. Soon, they had disappeared into the night and everybody breathed a sigh of relief.

Ray coolly straightened his tie.

'Tony, get us a cup of tea, son, will you? Two sugars, please.'

A young Tony Slade had shaken his head in admiration.

Ray Steele was a tough man, but also a fair one. He never hurt anybody that he had given a chance to walk. He was a true professional.

When Tony had come out of the forces, he had been forced back into door work, due to lack of working opportunities for ex-soldiers.

He had lived by Ray Steele's code and it had kept him in one piece on more occasions than he cared to remember.

In recent times, the skills that the military and Ray Steele had instilled in him had been invaluable. That training would always be with him, no matter how old he got, but he hoped that he would not have to resort to those skills any more.

Tony found that he was almost back at the restaurant. He planned to hit the shower and then look forward to a leisurely meal.

His life at present was pretty chilled for him, and he knew he should be feeling good about this. It had been a while since he had felt this relaxed, but he couldn't shake off a little niggling voice at the back of his mind saying that this was all too good to be true.

If Tony had learnt anything in his time on the planet, it was the fact that, when things were going well, life had a habit of sneaking up and biting you on the ass.

Inspector Steve Richmond's mobile sounded. He looked at the screen and saw that it was Harriet Grey calling. Richmond and his partner Marie were just on their way out for dinner. It was Marie's birthday.

'I need to take this, babe. I won't be a minute.'

Marie sighed. 'Well, be quick, Steve. We have the table booked for 8:30pm and they won't keep it.'

'It'll be fine. I won't be long. Promise.'

Marie had heard this many times before. Tonight, though, was special. As her birthday treat, they were dining at an exclusive restaurant, *Folly's*, in the affluent

Clifton area of Bristol. *Folly's* was owned by the television celebrity chef, Greg Folly, and had opened six weeks ago to rave reviews. Bookings there were like gold dust, but Richmond had pulled a few strings within the police ranks and secured a table for two.

Marie was over the moon, and it had certainly earned Richmond some brownie points. He hoped after the meal Marie would show him just how grateful she was when they got back home.

It was not the place Richmond would have gone out of choice. Plus, he thought Greg Folly was an overhyped smug prick, but Marie liked him, so he compromised. He certainly would need a leg over after paying the fucking prices on the menu.

Richmond walked into the kitchen and answered the call.

'Hi, Harriet. What have you got?'

'We got something from the mobile phone. The address book was still intact, and we looked at recent phone calls made. A number that crops up continually is an international number in America. It belongs to a Ruby Carter.'

The name rang no bells with Richmond.

'I take it there is more, Harriet?'

She laughed. 'God, no wonder you are a policeman. Well detected, Sherlock.'

'Bollocks. Get on with it. I have a reservation at Folly's waiting. It's Marie's birthday treat.'

'Wow, I am impressed, Steve and I had you down as a Burger King man.'

Steve chuckled. 'Come on. Spill it.'

Harriet continued, 'Ruby Carter is the daughter of Clint Carter. He was a famous and well-respected millionaire newspaper magnate in New York, recently deceased. Gary Carter was her brother. Ex-Marine.'

Richmond digested the news.

'Shit. I would say this Ruby Carter is going through a pretty traumatic time. What with losing her father and now her brother.'

Harriet agreed. 'I couldn't even begin to imagine.'

'Thanks, Harriet. Text me over her number and get the rest of your findings to Sergeant Drury asap.'

Harriett acknowledged this and rang off.

Richmond pocketed his phone and chewed over the information. What would the Carter family in New York want with Tony Slade? There was a tenuous military link, but Richmond sensed that this was not necessarily of major significance. He knew that he was going to have to make that call to New York himself.

Earlier that day, along with Sergeant Luke Drury, he had interviewed the two witnesses of the incident on the railway platform that had resulted in Gary Carter's death. Jake Preston and Alison Roache were boyfriend and girlfriend, both eighteen years old, and students at Bristol University. They seemed down-to-earth, level-headed kids when interviewed about the circumstances leading up to the murder. They were both still shook up about it, which was understandable.

Jake had explained about the problem with the gang and how Carter had sorted them out like the Terminator.

Richmond asked if he had spoken to them prior to or after the incident. Both had said no. He was just a stranger who had stepped in at the right moment.

Richmond then asked for descriptions of the three suspects, and which of them had pushed Carter to his death. He told them both to think carefully whether there was anything else that could be a clue to who these men were.

Jake shook his head, but then Alison interrupted and told them that the three lads had said that they were part of a gang. The something squad. Snow? Ice?

Drury interceded. He knew that the Ice Squad was a local gang known to the police in connection to drug running. They were mainly youngsters hired as mules to traffic drugs or pick up payments for the dealers.

She went on to say that they had also mentioned a man called Lenny Keating.

Both policemen knew Lenny Keating well. He was suspected of being one of the main players in the drug scene in Bristol, but was clever enough to hide behind owning a handful of legit businesses. His main ones were two nightclubs, *Roxy's* and *Snow White's*.

Keating had given the police the runaround for many years. Any convictions they had on him never stuck and he always walked free. He had many of the city's top brass in his pocket and on his payroll. Rumour had it that some of them were inside the police force.

Richmond knew Keating's background well. His old Governor DCI Wyatt had crossed swords with the man many times, but Keating had always got the better of him.

His story was not a conventional one. Keating was a clever bastard. University educated, he had graduated as a chartered accountant. Not your typical gangster, and not bad for a black boy born in the 1970s.

His parents were humble working-class people. His father was Irish, Dublin born. Francis Keating came to England in the 1960s and worked as a labourer building the new motorway system. His wife, Dorothy, was a

Jamaican who also came to England around the same time. She worked as a ward assistant in a local hospital and met Francis through her job, when he was admitted with an appendicitis, and their romance flourished.

Lenny was their first-born. Growing up with black and Irish parentage was no picnic in the 1970s. Political correctness did not exist. He learnt how to use his fists pretty quickly, but it was his smartness and intelligence that made him different.

His parents were proud that Lenny showed such talent at school and seemed to rise most of the time above the racism and bullying that was common in those years. Not only was he smart and could fight, he was also a good athlete and footballer. This made him popular. He had harboured ambitions to pursue one of these sports when he left school, but he had been pressurised by his parents to go to college and then university to have a 'real' career.

Back then, you did not argue with your parents.

Keating hated the whole accountancy thing. But then a tragic accident changed his life forever.

He had a younger brother named Ellis. He was close to him. Ellis was not blessed with Lenny's talent and struggled at school. Lenny helped him whenever he could, but Ellis became a bit wayward.

One night he stole a motorbike. Whilst riding it, he lost control and crashed into a wall. He died instantly.

Lenny was devastated, and his brother's death sent him over the edge. All his pent-up frustration and anger began to surface and he finally went off the rails himself. He jacked in his lucrative job and rebelled against his parents.

He got involved in a lot of the football hooliganism that was so ripe at that time, then he moved on to arranging disturbances and violence at demonstrations or rallies.

His capacity for violence got him noticed by a then old-school local villain, Harry Bowles. What also got him noticed was his sharp brain and organisational skills. Bowles offered Lenny a job.

Lenny worked as Harry's personal minder and rose up the ladder, becoming his trusted advisor where business was concerned.

When Harry died, Lenny took over the reins and flourished in the job.

Nobody fucked with Lenny Keating.

Now in his late forties, he was still a formidable man. His 6ft-plus frame, trademark shaven head, and scorpion tattoo on his neck, made people aware of exactly who he was. Richmond knew if Keating was involved in this incident, it was going to get nasty.

Both policemen had thanked the young couple for their help. The last question Richmond asked was if anybody else had been on the platform during this time, and they told him that there had been an elderly man sitting on one of the benches, but he had not been involved in anyway.

Richmond's thought process was broken by the voice of Marie.

'Steve, let's go. Can't you cut work loose for one evening?'

He headed towards the front door.

'Alright, babe. I am done. Let's go.'

As he headed to his car, he felt a bubble of adrenaline in his stomach. He felt something big was about to go down, and he wanted to be in it.

Chapter six

Lenny Keating let out a grunt and dropped the 35kg dumbbells onto the rubber matting. His deltoids screamed with the burn from the build-up of lactic acid in the muscles.

He regarded himself in the gym mirror. He was sitting on a reclined bench after completing three sets of eight-rep shoulder presses. He was looking pumped. Keating allowed himself a little grin of satisfaction.

He had completed his usual 6am workout at the *Raw Power* gym – a place of legendary status in Bristol. It was a hardcore lifting gym that housed some monsters. There was no CrossFit or yoga in here. Lenny was a director in the business along with the owner Dennis King, who back in the 1980s had been one-time British and Commonwealth powerlifting champion.

It was now 7:30am and the gym was getting a little busier. That is why he liked to get in early and get on with it. He did not like any distractions while he trained, or people talking shit.

Lenny stood up, grabbed his water bottle, and walked towards the changing rooms. Once in there, he opened his locker and grabbed hold of his shower kit. As he peeled off his wet t-shirt, one of the shower doors opened and out stepped a man.

Lenny recognised him. It was Ronnie Patterson – a regular here, and a competitive bodybuilder. He also worked the doors at the *Jungle Hut* club. Ronnie had his fingers in a few illegal pies, and the two men had done a bit of business before. Ronnie's speciality was selling firearms.

Lenny knew that in recent times Ronnie had been pulled in by the police after some fucking lunatic shot up the *Alpha Coffee House* last year with an Uzi. But they never got anything on him.

There was a mutual respect between the men, but Keating knew deep down that Patterson was afraid of him. He also knew that the other man was gay. This did not bother Keating, but he knew that many gay men were a little sensitive, especially about their looks, and he liked to play upon this.

Ronnie instantly saw Keating, and ran his eyes warily over the black man's solid physique.

'Watcha, Lenny. How you doing? You're looking ripped, man.'

Lenny grinned, displaying two gold incisors. 'You think so?'

Patterson walked over to his locker.

'Fuck yeah, Lenny. Awesome.'

Patterson stood with just his towel around his waist, slightly flexing his own muscles, waiting to see if Keating would return the compliment.

Keating wrapped a towel around himself and grabbed his shower bag.

'Thanks, Ronnie. I think you've put a bit of weight on around the stomach, man.'

Keating suppressed a smile as he entered a shower cubicle. He spied through a gap between the shower door and the wall, and saw Patterson immediately go to the full-length mirror on the wall and check out his stomach. He prodded and pinched the flesh, turning every which way and generally scrutinising his abs until his towel loosened and fell to the floor, leaving him standing in front of the mirror butt naked.

Keating turned on the shower and stepped under the water, grinning to himself and muttering, 'Fucking muppet,' under his breath.

When he finished showering and returned to the changing rooms, Patterson was gone. Keating dressed and then checked his phone. There was a voicemail. He listened to it. The message was from his right-hand man Joel Sterling.

'Hi, Lenny. I've just been speaking to Dave Rowlands down at *Dave's Café* and he told me apparently those little pricks Harvey Banks, Gaz Lewis, and Ethan Riggs have been in there spouting off about sorting out some dude at the railway station at the weekend. So, I looked online and found out that some American bloke was pushed off a platform at Temple Meads Station on Saturday night and killed.

'Dave then overheard that stupid cunt Harvey, apparently coked up to the tits, saying he pushed him to his death. The police are all over the crime scene, so I went to one of our sources and was told that a couple of witnesses said that they had trouble with three guys on the station. Apparently, then this American dude intervened and slapped the three of them about like little girls.

'Then the three stooges, after licking their wounds, told anybody in earshot that they were part of the Ice Squad gang and they worked for you. The police are yet to identify the individuals, but they are on it big time.'

Lenny Keating hung up the phone as the message ended. Suddenly, his mood darkened. He used the kids to ferry drugs around for him and they knew to keep their mouths closed. They got paid good money or scored a bit of gear. For that, they shut up.

But every now and then, some prick thought he was a gangster and overstepped the mark. Murdering a geezer was stepping way over the mark, especially if the trail led the police to his door. It was hassle that he did not need.

Lenny left the gym and walked over to his BMW 8 Coupé, opened the door and slipped behind the wheel. The car was new, and normally he would have sat, taking in the scent of the leather and running his hands over the smooth steering wheel for a few moments. But not today.

He phoned Joel Sterling. The man answered almost immediately. Keating cut straight to the chase.

'I got your message. Do you know if those pricks are still in the café?'

'I don't know, Lenny. I left that message over forty minutes ago. They might be?'

'Right, meet me outside *Roxy's* in fifteen minutes. Round up Big Will and Mad Micky as well, and get the Range Rover ready to go. Then we'll all go down to the café. We need to find these three before the police do.'

*

DI Richmond was driving into work. He sang along to the song on the radio: Wet Wet Wet's classic, *Love Is All Around*.

Indeed, it was, thought Richmond, *especially last night when the birthday meal had gone down so well and then so did Marie.*

He smiled at his joke. What a night to remember. Pity it did not happen more often. It had all certainly been worth the price in the end, but he doubted if he would be back at *Folly's* any time soon, unless he turned corrupt. Fuck, that menu was exorbitant.

His mind now turned to the case. He needed to nail some solid evidence down fast in relation to who had pushed Gary Carter to his death. Otherwise, Hardwick would be crawling up his ass. The connection with Slade would have to wait until he made some progress.

As he pulled up to a roundabout, he glanced to his right and all seemed clear. As he eased forward, a large black Range Rover and a BMW seemed to come out of nowhere, cut across him, then sped away.

Richmond jammed on the brakes and blasted his horn whilst shouting out 'pricks' to the disappearing vehicles. He wished that he had been given more time to catch their registrations.

Whoever were in those cars were sure in a hurry. Reckless bastards.

Suddenly, the rest of his journey was not so pleasurable.

Once at his desk with a proper cup of coffee in his hand, Richmond felt a lot better.

Sergeant Drury reported in that the CCTV at the railway station had picked up the altercation between Carter and the gang, although the camera angle was not brilliant. It did not pick up the pushing of the victim, but it did show a hooded youth running off the platform around the estimated time of the murder.

He also told Richmond that he had sent the footage to his computer.

Richmond thanked him.

Next, PC Garrett came in and told Richmond that she had done a little out-of-hours research on Gary Carter's family. There was a lot of stuff about them on social media. She related again that Gary's father had been Clint Carter, who had owned the *Manhattan News*. The recent news was all about his tragic death and his severely injured wife Katy.

Carter had been an incredibly popular figure who worked along with the city major Casper Nixon to run a purge on drug peddling and crime. Their daughter Ruby was now in line to run the company. She was apparently the apple of her daddy's eye and shared his same passion for the cause that was called the 'Great Clean-Up'.

Gary Carter had been the black sheep of the family. He had a long career in the US Marines, then drifted in and out of menial jobs, refusing the family's help or money. He had been off the radar until recently when he appeared after the family accident.

The background information was interesting, but it did not explain why Carter had ended up in Bristol, nor why he had all those newspaper clippings of Slade.

Richmond thanked Garrett. She went to walk away but hesitated.

'Gov, I just remembered something in the information about the Carters that may be relevant.'

Richmond looked up from his computer scene.

'Anything would help at the minute. What have you got?'

Garrett came back nearer to the desk.

'It concerns Katy Carter, the mother. Apparently, she was born in the UK and moved to America when she married.'

'Okay. So, what are you thinking?'

'Well, maybe that is the connection to why Gary Carter was in the UK.'

Richmond considered this for a moment.

'Thanks, Garrett. That might be significant.'

She turned to go, but Richmond spoke again.

'Wouldn't happen to know where in the UK she was born?'

Garrett consulted her notebook.

'Yeah, I have it here somewhere.'

She turned a few pages.

'Here we go. Durham. North East.'

Richmond's ears pricked up.

'Durham?'

'Yes, Gov. It's up by Sunderland, isn't it?'

Richmond nodded.

'That's right, and about eighteen miles from Newcastle. I think we may have just found our link. I need to speak to Ruby Carter. Good work, Garrett.'

Her face broke into a smile.

'Thank you, Gov.'

Richmond watched her leave his office. Garrett was showing good initiative and proving to become quite an asset to the investigation.

Richmond studied the footage from the station and the altercation that had taken place.

Carter had certainly handled the three yobs easily. The camera angles made it difficult to pick out the features of the gang, but Richmond felt he had seen the biggest youth around before. The thick gold chain and the baseball cap seemed familiar. He just could not place him at the moment, but it would come to him.

Finally, he watched the strutting figure with the hoodie walking off the platform and then running out of sight. It was definitely one of the three, but his features were obscured. Clever little fucker.

Richmond called Drury in again.

'Luke, see what we have on this Ice Squad gang, will you? And find out who the main movers and shakers are and where they hang out. Let's see if we can tie any of these jokers from the station in with them and put some names to faces.'

'Right away, Gov. I'll see what I can find out, but I suspect these particular little bastards have gone to ground.'

'Maybe,' answered Richmond, 'But see what you can find anyway.'

'Yes, of course,' replied Drury.

The black Range Rover and the BMW pulled up outside Dave's café. Lenny Keating got out of the BMW and slipped into the backseat of the Range Rover. He shut the door and regarded the three men inside.

'Gentlemen.'

The three men nodded.

Sitting next to Keating was Big Will. He could easily be mistaken for 'Iron' Mike Tyson, ex-heavyweight boxing champion of the world. The only major difference was that Big Will stood 6ft 6' compared to Tyson's 5ft 11'.

In the driver's seat was Joel Sterling, a good-looking, smartly dressed black man in his mid-20s. The man sitting next to him was white and in his forties. He was thick-set and built like a Pitbull. This was Mad Micky Stone.

'Right, Joel, you and Micky go in the café and see if the little scrotes are in there. If so, be discreet and bring them out. Will and I will wait here just in case they try to do a runner.'

Joel nodded, and both men got out of the Range Rover and entered the café. They scanned the place, but there was no sign of the men. Joel made his way to the counter. A young girl was wiping it down, oblivious to his presence.

'Hey, sweetheart. Dave about?' asked Joel.

The girl looked up. She blew a bubble with the gum she was chewing and regarded Joel. Her bored expression turned to one of interest when she regarded this good-looking dude. He was certainly a cut above the usual punter that frequented this establishment.

'Yeah, he's out the back cooking.'

'Can you tell him I want a word?'

'Okay, sure.'

She made to walk off in the direction of the kitchen when she suddenly stopped and turned around.

'Who shall I tell him it is that wants him?'

Joel flashed her one of his winning smiles.

'Joel. What's your name, sweetie?'

A slight blush came to the girl's face.

'It's Amy.'

Joel continued smiling.

'Very nice. I like the name Amy.'

Amy suddenly went all coy.

'I'll get Dave now.'

She disappeared into the kitchen.

Joel checked his appearance in a tarnished old mirror hanging on the wall beside a framed photograph of Robert De Niro and Al Pacino from the film *Heat*.

Dave Rowlands was a bit of a film buff and loved the old-school actors from the golden age of modern cinema.

'Hello, Joel. How are you?'

Joel turned to see Dave coming out of the kitchen, wiping his hands on a cloth. He wore an apron with an image of Marilyn Monroe on the front. It was stained with grease and oil. Dave was in his 60s, balding, and carried a bit too much weight around the mid-section – a result, no doubt, of sampling too much of his own cooking.

Joel stepped up close to the man.

'Alright, Dave. I'll come straight to the point. Do you know were Harvey Banks and his mates have gone?'

'They left about five minutes ago. I thought I heard them say they were going down to Bridge Park. I think they were planning on continuing their little party in private. They are already high as kites.'

'Okay, Dave. Nice one, my man.'

Joel pressed three twenties into the older man's hand.

'Usual, Dave. We never had this conversation.'

Dave nodded and headed back to the kitchen.

Joel jumped into the driver's seat and started the ignition.

'They are at Bridge Park. Planning on puffing some skunk, no doubt.'

Lenny nodded.

'Let's go gate-crash their party then. If the law finds them, they're going to straight away make the connection to me, and that can't happen. Understand?'

The three men all agreed.

Keating got out of the vehicle.

'I'll follow you in my motor.'

'This is some good shit. I am fucking floating.'

Harvey Banks slumped back on the bench in the brick shelter of the park. The place smelt of stale piss and vomit, but it was tucked out of the way of prying eyes. The floor was littered with empty beer cans, Styrofoam takeaway dishes, and a couple of used condoms. The walls of the shelter were covered in years of graffiti work.

Gaz Lewis and Ethan Riggs were also sprawled on the bench. Both had stupid grins on their faces. Their eyes were glazed.

'What a fucking life, boys. While all those other losers out there are working in their dead-end jobs, we're here doing good laughing grass. We have money in our pockets, and we are the fucking Ice Squad,' continued Banks.

Gaz Lewis stood up on unsteady legs and flexed his biceps. His right wrist and forearm were in plaster from his encounter at the railway station.

'Yeah. No-one fucks with the Ice Squad and gets away with it. We are bulletproof.'

'Here, Harvey.'

It was Ethan Riggs talking through slurred words. He was also speaking through a broken nose that had left him with two black eyes.

'Do you think the police have got anything on us and that American dude? What about CCTV on the station?'

Harvey scratched at a pimple on his chin that was giving him a few problems.

'We are good, man. A mate of mine, Billy Stiles, worked there recently until he got the push for nicking chocolate out of the vending machines, and I have it on good authority that the cameras are useless. Some don't work or aren't positioned right. Plus, we all had hoodies or caps on. We could be fucking anybody. Don't sweat it. We are good.'

Riggs grinned.

'Well, amen to that, brother.'

He took another draw on the spliff and passed it to Gaz.

'You're a fucking nutter, Harvey. I mean, a right fuckin' looney tune.'

Harvey laughed, then stood up and took a theatrical bow.

'Fuck that prick on the station. He had it coming, and we are sweet.'

Suddenly, a shadow loomed over the shelter. The boys looked up to see the eclipse that was Big Will.

'Fuck, Will. I nearly shat myself with you creeping up like that,' said Harvey.

Will walked into the shelter. He wrinkled his nose at the odour.

'Is it the shelter or you lot that smells of piss?'

'Yeah, very funny, Will,' replied Gaz.

Big Will regarded the three youths with disdain.

'Boss wants to see you boys now. He's across the road.'

The boys regarded each other.

'It's a job, is it, Will?' asked Gaz.

Will walked out of the shelter.

'The boss will explain. Come on. Let's not keep him waiting.'

Lenny Keating was sitting in the Range Rover. He saw Will and the three boys coming. He drew in a deep breath and looked at the other two men in the vehicle.

'Right, let's not spook the fuckers. Otherwise, they're going to run. Let me do the talking.'

Both men nodded that they understood.

Lenny got out of the vehicle. As the boys approached, his face split into a huge grin.

'Well, here are the main men.'

The boys nervously regarded him.

Banks spoke.

'Everything alright, boss?'

Keating spread his hands.

'Everything is cool, Harvey. Unless you know otherwise?'

Harvey smiled uncertainly.

'Me? No, boss. I am all good.'

Harvey was craning his neck to see who else was in the Range Rover, but the tinted windows prevented him.

'Well, that's good to know. I have a little job to discuss with you.'

Keating saw the three immediately relax.

'What is it, boss?' asked Gaz.

Keating regarded the boy.

'What happened to your wrist, Gaz? Been pulling your wanger too much?'

The boy's face coloured up as everybody laughed.

'No, I punched the bag wrong down the gym. That's all.'

Keating nodded.

'What about you, Riggs? You look like a fucking panda. Been in a bit of a scrap, have we?'

'Bit of heavy sparring down the gym. It's nothing,' Riggs mumbled.

Keating looked at Harvey Banks.

'What about you? Any injuries?'

'No, Lenny. Like I said, I am all good.'

'Well, I didn't know you boys were so keen on your fitness, being pot and coke-heads and all that.'

'Yeah, we do a few drugs recreationally like, but we are always working out as well. Aren't we, boys?' lied Harvey.

'Oh yeah, I can see that. Well, that's good, because we can discuss the job I have lined up for you down at the *Raw Power* gym. It will be discreet there. Right, jump in the Range Rover then, lads. Will, you come with me. I'll see you boys all down there.'

As Lenny Keating pulled away, he saw the boys get into the Range Rover. They all looked nervous, especially Harvey Banks.

....

'Well, here we all are then. Altogether. Nice and cosy like.'

Lenny Keating was standing in the large backroom of the *Raw Power* gym. This area was off-limits to the customers. Only Lenny or Dennis King and a few invited friends even knew it existed.

Gaz Lewis coughed nervously.

'So, what's the job, Lenny? Is it a bit of drug running or collecting?'

Lenny Keating's face broke into that huge toothy grin again. It reminded Lewis of a great white shark heading in for the kill.

'Not so fast, Gaz my man. Before we discuss that, I want you to explain to me what the fuck happened on the railway station the other night with this American? I am surprised you didn't think to mention it to me.'

Lewis glanced in the direction of his two buddies.

Keating continued, 'Before you say anything, think carefully. Do not treat me like a fucking idiot, and do not bullshit me. Are we clear?'

Lewis swallowed hard and spilt the story. When he had finished, there was silence. This time, when Keating spoke, the menace was obvious in his voice.

'So, Harvey, you little no-good fucker. You thought you would take it on yourself to be the fucking Terminator, did you?'

Harvey went to speak, but Joel Sterling grabbed his arm. The look he gave him told Harvey to be silent. Keating moved closer to the younger man.

'Well, you have brought the fucking heat sniffing around, and they will be trying to put two and two together and coming up with five. They will be looking for that connection between you and me. You have been a complete prick.'

Harvey backed away. Fear showed in his eyes.

'Lenny, I am sorry. I just did it on the spur of the moment. A rush of blood to the head. I didn't think. The geezer fucked us up a bit. I wanted to teach him a lesson. Nobody will know it's us.'

Keating leaned right into Harvey Banks' face.

'Nobody will know. Is that right? First, you have been down *Dave's Café,* shouting it from the rooftops, and second, there are two witnesses on the railway station that heard you say you worked for me.'

Harvey's face paled.

'I'm sorry, Lenny. I didn't think. I was high. I—'

Keating cut him dead.

'Damn right you didn't think. You killed a man on my patch. You are a fucking liability. Nobody does that sort of thing without my say-so.'

Keating then pointed at Lewis.

'And you are a useless prick for taking him on. I trusted you.'

The big man moved with surprising speed and drove a punch into Lewis's stomach. The boy folded to the ground like a cheap suit.

Ethan Riggs turned to run, but Big Will picked him up in a bear hug, like a baby, and then slammed him into the wall. The lad slid down it to a seated position, any fight suddenly gone out of him.

Harvey Banks was now held by Joel and Mad Micky. He whimpered his apologies.

Keating looked him in the eye.

'There is CCTV footage, so the police will finally find out it was you, and then that will lead them to me.

They will be poking around in my business, and that can't happen. I will not and cannot let it happen. I only use you twats because you're cheap and easily bought. It also saves me getting my hands dirty. But when you work for me, there are fucking rules to follow. You have broken them and jeopardised my business. As from now, you are surplus to requirement, boys.'

Lenny Keating looked at his men and nodded. They reached into their pockets and produced earplugs, which they all, including Keating, stuck into their ears. Banks looked confused and then frightened.

Suddenly, Keating reached into his inside pocket and pulled out a small, sleek black gun and pointed it towards the boy's head. Banks paled.

'This, my friend, is a Walther CCP 9-shot semi-automatic. Little, easy to conceal, but fucking deadly.'

'Fuck. Please, Lenny. Don't—'

The gun retorted and a bullet hit Banks between the eyes. He was dead before he hit the floor. Keating looked across the room at the other two boys and aimed the pistol towards them. They both scrambled to their feet, fear fuelling their fight or flight responses.

Keating pulled the trigger, but there was no retort of gunfire. The gun had jammed. Keating tried again, but nothing happened. In the confusion, Gaz Lewis and Ethan Riggs ran for their life towards the fire door at the back of the room.

Big Will tried to make a grab for them, but they were too fast for the big man.

As the door neared, both boys prayed that when they pushed down on the crash bar, it would open. They were in luck. They spilled out into an alley behind the gym and sped off. They could hear angry voices shouting behind them.

Gaz glanced over his shoulder to see Mad Micky levelling a gun in their direction, but Lenny Keating appeared beside him and knocked down the man's arm. It was far too risky to let off a firearm outside in such a public area.

Both boys scaled a large gate at the end of the alleyway and were gone.

When Keating and Micky returned to the gym, Big Will and Joel were already unrolling a large plastic sheet for disposal of Harvey Banks's body.

They both looked up at Keating. The big man's face was contorted in rage.

'Those pair of wankers got away. I want the whole area scoured for them. I want them found asap. I am going to skin their fucking hides. Find them. Understand?'

'Okay, Lenny. I am on it, man. We'll find them. No sweat,' said Joel.

Chapter seven

Detective Inspector Steve Richmond had been called to a morning meeting with Chief Superintendent Hardwick.

Hardwick wanted the chapter and verse on any updates in the murder case of Gary Carter. Now that they knew Carter's family background and their standing in the New York Community, pressure from the top was coming down to find his killers. Hardwick had impressed on Richmond that even the US President had taken an active interest in the case and had apparently been talking to the British Prime Minister.

The case was now bigger than they had first imagined.

Richmond had given Hardwick a progress report, but chose to exclude the newspaper clipping found of Slade and his gathering suspicions of a connection. He knew if he remotely let his superior know he was on the trail of Slade again, he would shut him down. Hardwick was only interested in keeping the heat off his own ass.

Richmond assured Hardwick that he would keep him updated, and this seemed to satisfy the man for the moment.

Now, he had just come off the phone to the American Embassy in London, giving them the details of the death of Gary Carter and informing them that he needed to speak with Gary's sister Ruby urgently.

Consular officer Bradley Kinkade told Richmond that he would ask a member of the New York police department to deliver the news of the death in person to Ruby Carter. He stressed to Richmond that anybody dealing with this matter had better tread carefully, as the woman had been through an incredibly traumatic time of late, and more bad news could tip her over the edge. He told Richmond that, as soon as the police were done at their end, he would be able to speak with her.

....

At 5pm New York time, Kinkade spoke to Detective Wes Miller.

At 6:20pm, Miller went to Ruby's office at the *Manhattan News* to break the tragic news to her. He was a veteran of many such calls.

He was shown into her office. Ruby Carter was at her desk, finishing off some paperwork.

'Hello, Detective. This is an unexpected police visit. I was just finishing up for the day. Is this something to do with my parents' accident?'

Miller gestured towards the empty chair in front of her desk.

'May I?'

'Yes, of course,' replied Ruby.

Miller sat down and showed her his badge.

'No, this is nothing to do with that. This is another matter.'

'Very intriguing. I take it a detective wouldn't be making a personal call regarding the outstanding parking ticket I got the other day.'

'No, ma'am. This is something more serious. Can you confirm that you have a brother named Gary Carter?'

Ruby suddenly felt a sickening feeling in the pit of her stomach.

'Yes, I do. Why? Is he okay?'

'I have some bad news for you. I am sorry to inform you that your brother is dead.'

Ruby Carter felt as if the room was closing in on her. She reached for the half empty glass of water on her desktop with trembling hands, and took a few sips. She heard the detective's voice continue, but she found it hard to focus.

She heard something about England, a railway platform, and being pushed. It all faded in and out like a bad radio signal.

'Ma'am, are you okay?'

Ruby broke down in a flood of tears. Things had just gone from bad to worse.

Finally, she regained a little of her composure and she asked the detective, 'Tell me again, please. What happened to him? How did he die?'

Over the next ten minutes, Detective Wes Miller exposed the details of her brother's death. He also gave her the number of consular officer Kinkade who was ready to help her in any way he could. Finally, he told her that a Detective Inspector Steve Richmond of Bristol CID, who was handling the case in the UK, would be contacting her soon with some questions.

Ruby listened in silence, trying to process the information, but also trying to come to terms with the set of tragedies that had befallen her family in recent weeks. Her world was literally crashing down around her.

Gary dead. Gary, who had survived numerous conflicts in the Marines. Gary, a fighter. Yet in recent days, in her bones, she had felt something was not right.

The circumstances of his death seemed so pointless. A tragedy. Some fucking low-life that was not fit to even lace her brother's boots had done this and, up to now, walked away scot free.

When Detective Miller left her office, after she declined the offer of anybody's company or support, the tears came again. All the emotion of losing her brother and father, and the stress of her mother still in hospital, hit home hard. She suddenly felt alone.

Then the guilt came.

Why had she sent Gary looking for this Tony Slade? What good would it do to rake up the past? What had she been thinking of? If she hadn't have sent Gary to the UK, then he wouldn't have been on the goddamn railway station in the first place.

In her desk drawer, she found the half empty bottle of Jack that she kept for special clients. She was not usually a bourbon drinker, but this evening was an exception. She pressed the button on her desk phone and told her personal assistant Martha to go on home, as she planned to work late.

She then locked the office door and took the bottle and a glass to the sofa. She kicked off her shoes and poured two fingers of bourbon into the glass and downed it in one gulp. She coughed as the liquid burned a trail down her throat to her stomach.

She drank on until late, going over everything in her mind, time and time again. Eventually, she curled up on the sofa, drunk and exhausted, sleep blissfully taking her away from all her troubles.

Ruby awoke at 6:30am. She felt stiff and cold, and her head felt like it was stuffed with cotton wool. She gingerly got to her feet, swaying slightly. She steadied herself and made her way to her office restroom.

Ruby switched on the light. The sudden brightness hurt her eyes. She ran water in the basin and splashed it on her face. Suddenly, she felt nauseous, and moved to the toilet where she dropped to her knees and was violently sick.

After finishing, she sat on the cold tiled floor for ten minutes before summoning the energy to get up, shed her clothes, and get in the shower.

When she exited it, she felt a lot better. She would not be hitting the bourbon again for a while.

Ruby dried her hair, applied her make-up, and changed into fresh underwear, shirt, and suit which she always kept on site. Her next priority was heading across the block to *Starbucks*. The inside of her mouth tasted like old leather, even after brushing her teeth twice.

Suddenly, the previous night's conversation with Detective Miller came flooding back and her heart felt heavy. She wondered how she could break the terrible news to her mum. For now, she could not even think of it. Her mother was far too ill to have another shock. It could wait. Pushing the thought to the back of her mind, she left her office.

One large black americano later, Ruby was beginning to feel a little more human. She returned to her office after a long walk and headed straight to Freddie Golding's office to tell him the terrible news.

Freddie was understandably shocked. The loss of his close friend and confidant Clint Carter had been a tough blow to take. Now this was just unbelievable.

Freddie was Ruby's godfather, and felt wholly responsible for her. He urged Ruby to take some time out from work, fearing for her mental state, but she told him that she would only be moping at home and needed the distraction of being in the office.

As a compromise, she accepted his offer of the company liaising with the consul to bring home her brother's body and organise the funeral arrangements. The conversation ended by Golding telling her that he would help her and the company out in anyway needed. She only had to say.

Ruby returned to her office. She felt a little better for telling Freddie, but still found it hard to concentrate. Her thoughts were in turmoil. Within the last few months, the life she knew had literally fallen apart at the seams. She did not know what to expect next.

Was the death of her brother connected to Tony Slade, or was it just a terrible coincidence?

At 2.30pm UK time, DI Richmond got the go-ahead to speak to Ruby Carter. He was put through to her office phone by her personal assistant. The phone was answered immediately.

'Hello. Ruby Carter speaking."

Richmond leant forward in his chair and glanced up to make sure that his office door was closed.

'Hello, Ms Carter? My name is Detective Inspector Steve Richmond, Bristol CID in England. Can we talk?'

'Yes, of course. I was expecting you to call.'

'May I just say how sorry I am for your loss and your recent tragic events. I can't imagine how you must feel.'

'Thank you, Inspector... I'm sorry, what did you say your name was?'

'Detective Inspector Steve Richmond.'

'My apologises for being a bit vague. I am still struggling to come to terms with the news, but please talk away and I will help you in any way I can.'

Richmond went on to explain the full circumstances surrounding her brother's death, and told her that they were actively pursuing some leads.

He explained that his team in the UK were looking into a gang called the Ice Squad, made up of youngsters that frequented the south of the city. Many of them had been arrested for vandalism, petty theft, intimidation, and robbery with violence. They were also allegedly known to run drugs and collect payments for a Lenny Keating, but the police had no hard evidence as yet to back this up.

The main man in the gang was a Gaz Lewis. Two of his cronies were his right-hand boys, named Harvey Banks and Ethan Riggs. These three would liaise with many other kids, usually younger than themselves, to help out on runs. Many of these kids were doing this from their bikes. They knew their patch inside out and also knew every shortcut, back alley, and escape route to avoid the police.

He suspected these were the lads in the station's CCTV footage, especially as Lewis had a liking for chunky gold jewellery. The only problem was that nobody seemed to know where these three were at present, which did not help. Their disappearance seemed no coincidence in the light of the murder.

Richmond then asked Ruby why Gary had been in England and in Bristol.

She explained the whole story about what had happened to her parents and her mother's disclosure about her real father. She then revealed that Gary had been looking for this man, because she wanted to meet him.

Richmond asked her the man's name, but he already suspected the answer. When she replied Tony Slade, he had now solved the mystery of the newspaper cutting in Gary Carter's pocket.

Well, what a turn-up for the books. Tony Slade had a daughter he knew nothing about. It looked as if Slade's past was going to once more pop up and kick him in the balls.

Suddenly, Richmond began to see a plan forming in his head. A plan to get Slade out of hiding and nail his ass once and for all.

He asked if it was possible for Ruby to fly to the UK in order to identify her brother's body and tie up some details and paperwork.

She told him that Freddie Golding, the paper's assistant director, had expressed a wish to do this on her behalf. Richmond lied that the US Consulate was dragging its heels on this matter and if she personally made the identity and signed the forms in person, it would certainly speed up the process of getting her brother's body flown back to New York.

Ruby readily agreed; she was desperate for closure on this matter. Two burials of loved ones so close to each other was too much to bear, and she just wanted it over with as soon as possible. She told him she would make the necessary flight arrangements and get back to him. They exchanged private mobile numbers.

Richmond's ploy had worked.

When he got off the phone, he sat thinking for a moment. He needed a little help to hatch his plan and he knew the ideal person to do that. He scrawled the address book in his mobile phone until he found the number he wanted. Then, he pressed dial.

After a couple of rings, the call connected

'Hello, stranger. What can I do for you then?' asked a female voice.

Richmond smiled to himself. 'Hello, sexy. How's life in the capital?'

'Oh, you know, busy, noisy, and full of foreigners.'

Richmond laughed.

'Just like here then.'

'So, Steve, what's up?'

'Well, I'm in the need of the specialist skills of Susie Rawlings, newspaper reporter extraordinaire. Can we meet up and talk? I've got some information that I think is going to interest you.'

'I'm intrigued. I have to come down to Bristol this weekend to pick up a few bits and pieces I've had in storage since my move. We could catch up then if you like?'

'That sounds ideal, Susie. Give me a ring later to arrange a meeting place.'

'Okay, Steve. No clue to what this is about then?' she asked.

'Let's save it until we can talk face-to-face. It will be worth it. I promise. See you soon.'

Richmond rang off.

*

At the other end, Susie Rawlings put her phone down.

She had not seen Steve Richmond since DCI John Wyatt's funeral, other than a fleeting hospital visit when Richmond was first admitted after his fall. She had heard that he had recently gone back to work. What did he have up his sleeve to want to meet face-to-face after all this time?

Chapter eight

'So, Steve. What is this all about? It all seems very secretive,' said Susie Rawlings.

DI Richmond took a sip of his coffee and regarded her.

The London lifestyle seemed to be suiting Susie. Since he last saw her, she must have lost 5kgs. She also sported a new hairstyle, and the Gucci handbag sitting on the table beside her didn't come cheap. She was looking good. She certainly cut a better figure than the forlorn and rain-soaked one on the island of Graig O Mor a year or so back.

They were seated in *Costa* in Bristol city centre. It was busy, but Richmond had managed to secure a table in the corner which was reasonably secluded.

'I have a story for you, if you want it?'

Susie stirred her latte.

'Go on. I'm listening.'

'Did you read the story about the American shoved off the railway platform down here recently?'

'Christ. Yes, I did. And do you know what? Apparently, he came into the offices of *The West Country Express* a little while back, asking for me.'

'Did he indeed? Did you know him?' asked Richmond.

'No. Never heard of him,' Susie replied. 'Matt Sloan took his number but then forgot to give it to me. It was only after he read about the death himself that it jogged his memory, and he contacted me. But by then, it was too late.'

'Maybe not Susie,' said Richmond.

Susie looked confused. 'What do you mean, Steve?'

'This Gary Carter was from New York, and he was the son of Clint Carter, the former owner of the *Manhattan News*,' Richmond told her.

'Jesus, I never made the connection. Shit. How terrible that both father and son are dead within weeks of each other,' replied Susie. 'Are their deaths connected? Is that what this is all about?'

Richmond shook his head.

'No, that piece of information isn't the story.'

Susie leaned forward in her seat and tore open a sachet of sugar for her drink.

'Okay then. I am all ears.'

'Gary had a sister called Ruby, but I have found out that Clint Carter wasn't her real father.'

'Okay, Steve. So, who was?'

Richmond smiled.

'Cross your legs, sweetheart. Her real dad is none other than Tony fucking Slade.'

Susie stopped stirring her coffee.

'You are kidding me, right?'

'No joke, Susie. It is one-hundred percent genuine. Straight from the horse's mouth, so to speak.

Richmond then went on to tell Susie the whole story.

When he finished, Susie Rawlings sat back in her chair and expelled her breath.

'Wow. That is some story, Steve. So, where do I fit in?'

'You, Susie my dear, are going to write a front-page exclusive for *The Daily News*, seeing you are a big-shot reporter these days.'

It was true. Before the incident on Graig O Mor island with Tony Slade, her career had been going down the pan. But being there and witnessing the situation that had unfolded, Susie had got the front-page scoop for the newspaper she was writing for at the time: *The West Country Express*.

On the back of that, she had received many accolades and been headhunted by the bigger mainstream tabloids. Very soon, she was living a different life in London, working for *The Daily News* as one of their top correspondents. Her career had certainly taken a turn for the better.

'Well, that's great news, Steve, but I guess this comes with a price?'

Richmond laughed.

'Believe it or not, it would be you that is doing me a favour.'

Susie raised her eyebrows.

'No, seriously. You get that news on the front page and online, and I am fairly sure wherever Slade is holed up, he will see it. If I know him, it will lure him out of hiding to find Ruby Carter and confirm the authenticity of the claim that he's her father,' continued Richmond.

'How can it benefit you if Slade goes swanning off to America to find this girl? You won't know if he is there or not?' asked Susie.

DI Richmond drained his coffee cup.

'Ah well, I have asked Ruby Carter to come over to Bristol to sort out some "paperwork" for the transferral of her brother's body. I plan to keep her here a little while. Now, you make sure to mention the fact she is visiting the UK in your article, and I think Slade might come looking.'

'That's a long shot, Steve,' remarked Susie. 'Do you think he is in Europe?'

'I have always suspected that he was. When we were investigating the "Coffee Shop Massacre", in amongst the evidence was the story of the extremely violent death of a Ray Steele who lived in Lanzarote. On further investigation, we found out that he originally came from Durham and had been an old friend of Slade's from his days of working on the doors.

'Steele was found dead, nailed to the floor gangland-style. This also tied up with the possibility that Slade was connected to North East gangster Kenny Robbins. Steele owned a bar, and I believe that Slade may have gone there as a quick place to skip to until the heat died down.

'I was up for pursuing this theory after the Governor's death,' Richmond went on, 'but old Chief Superintendent Hard Dick had other ideas, and told me the case was cold and to move on. But I can't forget that bastard Slade. I still want to see him behind bars.'

Susie reached across the table and touched Richmond's arm.

'I still miss John myself. He was a good copper and a good man.'

Richmond nodded. 'Thanks, Susie.'

The moment passed and Richmond rose from the table.

'So, can you get the piece in the paper by Monday?'

'I think that can be arranged,' replied Susie.

'Great. Remember you didn't hear it from me.'

They parted company but promised to keep each other updated on any developments.

When DI Richmond got back into his car, his phone sounded.

It was a message from Ruby Carter. She was flying into Bristol on Sunday. Her flight would land at Bristol Airport at 4pm.

Richmond texted back that he would be waiting to meet her. As he started the car up, he felt a tingle of excitement in his belly – something that he had not felt for some time.

DI Steve Richmond waited at the Bristol Airport arrivals gate, accompanied by PC Debbie Garrett. Richmond thought that bringing Garrett would make things a little less intimidating for Ruby Carter.

It was 4:15pm on Sunday afternoon, and the flight from JFK Airport had landed on time a quarter of an hour ago.

Earlier, Susie Rawlings had contacted him to say the newspaper piece was cleared for the front-page tomorrow morning. Richmond's plan was gradually taking shape.

The doors of the arrival gates slid smoothly open and Richmond looked out for Ruby. He had downloaded her recent image from a social media site, and PC Garrett held a photo image in her hand.

A stream of people moved through the doors, and after five minutes or so, Richmond spotted her. He ran appraising eyes over her.

Ruby Carter was an attractive woman. She was in good shape. Not overweight. Her strawberry blonde hair was tied back in a black ribbon. She wore a pair of faded blue jeans tucked into black ankle boots. She also wore a red jacket over an expensive looking black silk blouse. She looked cool and assured, wheeling a blue suitcase with a holdall resting on top of it.

Richmond came forward and produced his ID badge.

'Ms Carter, I am Detective Inspector Steve Richmond, and this is Police Constable Debbie Garrett. Welcome to the UK. Follow me and I will get you to the car. Your hotel is not too far from here.'

Ruby Carter said hello to both police officers, and they all moved off towards the exit.

Richmond's car pulled up outside the entrance of the Ravenscroft Hotel in Bristol city centre of Bristol. It was a grand five-star accommodation which Richmond had managed to square away with Superintendent Hardwick on the police expenses sheet, by convincing him that Ruby Carter could be a vital help in catching her brother's killers.

Once checked in, Richmond informed her that he would be back in the morning at 10am to pick her up and take her to the morgue to make a formal identification of her brother's body, although fingerprint and dental records had already confirmed the body to most certainly be that of Gary Carter. Even though the injuries that caused his death were horrific, his face had miraculously remained essentially unscathed.

Before he left, Ruby asked Richmond if there was any more news on her brother's murderers. He embarrassingly told her that there were no further breakthroughs as yet, but he assured her that they were doing all they could to find out who had done this. Richmond disclosed that the lead on the Ice Squad and Lenny Keating was still the one they were pursuing.

'You don't suspect my brother of being involved with drugs, do you?' asked Ruby.

Richmond shook his head.

'No, not all. We believe his death was the result of an untimely altercation with these guys. If we can track them down, then we will know for sure.'

'Well, please keep me updated, Detective Inspector.'

'Yes, of course.'

Richmond coughed awkwardly.

'Ms Carter, can I ask you one more thing?'

'Yes, what is it?'

'The man your brother came looking for, who you say is your biological father. Do you know anything about him?'

Ruby eyed the policeman suspiciously.

'Only what I pulled down from the web. Why do you ask?'

'I know this is probably not what you need to hear, with everything else that has been happening, but he is wanted by the police here in the UK.'

'What for, may I ask?'

DI Richmond gestured towards an empty sofa across the reception area. 'Shall we take a seat for a moment?'

When they were seated, Richmond gave the background that he had on Slade, and the encounters the police had had with him in the past. When he had finished, Ruby was silent. It was a lot to take in.

'I am sorry to unload all this on you, but I have a suspicion that Slade may try to contact you. If he does, I would hope you would do the right thing and let us know.'

Ruby remained silent.

Richmond asked if she wanted PC Garrett to keep her company, but Ruby declined. She told them that she was going to order room service and get an early night.

*

When the police left, Ruby made her way to the lifts, chewing over the information she had just heard. It was hard to associate the man that Richmond had spoken about as the one her mum fondly remembered, but it had been an awfully long time ago and she had told them he could be prone to fits of violence.

By her mum revealing the secret about this Tony Slade, she seemed to have opened a whole Pandora's box. But being from a newspaper background, Ruby was astute enough to know that there were always two sides to every story. For now, she decided to reserve judgement on Slade.

Richmond dropped PC Garrett off at the police station and quickly popped in to speak with Sergeant Luke Drury. He found him at his desk, just finishing off a phone call. For a moment, he looked surprised to see Richmond back, but then he regained his composure.

'Ah, Gov. Just the man I wanted to see,' he said.

'What have you got for me, Luke? Please tell me we have something positive.' Richmond took a seat.

'Well, I have tracked down an ex-member of the Ice Squad gang, a Liam Crooks. He did a stretch in prison but now works at a local hospice. A reformed character these days, but still has his ear to the ground, so to speak,' said Drury, 'I spoke with him earlier today. He told me that the word is that nobody has seen Banks, Lewis or Riggs for the best part of a week, which is unusual as they are always about on their turf keeping tabs on things. Nobody knows where they are. The word is that they're running scared.'

'I thought you had some good news here, Luke,' interrupted Richmond.

'I'm getting to it, Steve. This Crooks said that, when he was part of the gang before doing time, they used to have a hideout down by the docks. He never went there, but he reckoned it was an old boating warehouse down behind where the SS *Great Britain* is moored.'

'Does this warehouse have a name?'

'That, we don't know, but Crooks thinks that, if they are hiding from the heat, they could be there. They must also have somebody working as a go-between from their hideout to their business ground. They can't risk anybody else muscling in on their territory.'

'Okay, Luke. So, do we know who this go-between is then?'

'Crooks said that when he was part of the set-up, the go-between usually was Kirsty Byfield, a girlfriend of Gaz Lewis.'

Richmond stood up. 'Have you an address for this Kirsty Byfield?'

'That's the good news. Last known address, Mounthill Gardens, Flat 807.'

Richmond knew the block of flats. They were situated in a less upmarket district of Bristol, and right in the Ice Squad's stomping ground.

'Good work, Luke. Get yourself around there sharpish, and bring Garrett. I am heading home. Let me know what you get, okay?

Drury reached for his jacket on the back of his seat.

'Will do, Gov.'

An hour later, Richmond answered his phone to Luke Drury, to be told that Kirsty's mother Elsie Byfield had answered the door of Flat 807 and told them that Kirsty was out, she did not know where she was, or what time she was coming back. She went on to say that she was not her keeper. Kirsty was eighteen and could come and go as she pleased. All in all, it had been a frosty reception.

Richmond suspected that as soon as the two policemen left, Elsie would have been straight on the phone to her daughter.

Richmond told Drury and Garrett to call it a day and to pursue it again tomorrow.

Kirsty Byfield would soon show up. He had no doubt about that, and then he would see where she would lead them.

He turned the volume on his TV back up again and reached for his G&T.

Chapter nine

'Here she comes. I knew she would be back. Just like a bad fucking penny.'

Sergeant Luke Drury straightened up in the car. Next to him, PC Debbie Garrett did the same.

They had decided to get up at the crack of dawn on Monday and go back to Mounthill Gardens to wait for Kirsty Byfield, gambling that her mother had contacted her after last night's visit.

Their hunch had paid off. Once again, social media was great at providing a face to a name, and they both recognised the features of Kirsty Byfield.

As she got closer, her features became clearer. Jet black hair pulled back severely to her scalp. Heavy black eye make-up and ruby red lipstick. She was dressed all in black, sporting a pair of high ankle Dr Marten boots. She glanced furtively around. Obviously, she had been informed about their previous visit.

'How do you want to do this, Serg?' asked Debbie Garrett.

'We will let her go in the flat. Otherwise, she is likely to do a runner.'

Both waited until Kirsty entered the building and they saw her appear on the eighth-floor balcony, looking over it briefly to check the surroundings below.

Just then, DS Drury saw the milkman pull up outside the flats.

'Well, well, well. Thank goodness the milkman isn't totally extinct these days.'

With that, he jumped out of the car and approached him. A few minutes later, he came back to the car with two pints of milk.

Garrett regarded him.

'Planning on grabbing some Crunchy Nut Corn Flakes, are we?'

'No, Garrett. This is our way into the flat. I just had a little chat with the milkman, who told me that he delivers every day to 807, and today he knocks the door for his money. But today, it will be us knocking. Well, it will be me. You are going to head around the back of the building and check out any possible rear exits in case our girl legs it.'

Both police officers got out of the car and headed towards the flats.

....

When Kirsty Byfield entered the flat, her mother instantly appeared at the foot of the stairs.

'Thank God you are back, Kirsty. What do the police want you for? You haven't been getting mixed up with that Gaz Lewis and his cronies again, have you? I told you to stay away from them. They are rubbish.'

Kirsty took off her coat and threw it over the bannister then pushed her way past her mother.

'Not now, Mum. I'm knackered. I need some sleep.'

'Where have you been all night?' asked Elsie Byfield.

She was answered by the shutting of her daughter's bedroom door. Elsie sighed and walked into the kitchen. She reached for the kettle and filled it with water before plugging it in. Going to the fridge, she cursed under her breath as she saw the empty milk bottle. It was then that there was a knock on the door. Shit, who was that at this time of the morning.

Elsie walked into the hallway. 'Yes, who is it?'

'Milkman, Mrs Byfield,' replied a voice.

Elsie breathed a sigh of relief.

'Just leave it on the step, please.'

'Will do, but I need paying today for the week.'

Elsie cursed again and went to the kitchen for her purse. She came back into the hall.

'Okay, I'm on my way,' she called.

When she opened the door, for a moment she could not understand why Stan the milkman was not standing there, but instead a younger man in a suit. Then suddenly, it came flooding back to her. She made to shut the door, but DS Drury stuck his boot in it, jamming the closure.

'Morning, Mrs Byfield. I just saw Kirsty come home. I would like that word with her now, please.'

Elsie Byfield was flushed and caught off guard, but recovered enough to say, 'She's in bed asleep.'

Drury remained patient.

'Then please wake her. I doubt she can be asleep that fast. She only came in minutes ago.'

The woman regarded him and then turned towards the staircase, but Drury was ahead of her.

'Let's not shout and startle her, shall we? I'll just come in and speak to her myself.'

Elsie Byfield stared at him with hatred in her eyes, but she relented and let Drury in.

As he entered the hall, Kirsty appeared at the bottom of the stairs.

'Who is it, Mum?'

She saw Drury and tried to run to the kitchen, but Drury was quicker. He blocked her way and flashed his warrant card.

'DS Drury. I would like a word with you, Kirsty Byfield. We can do it here or we can do it down the station. It's your call.'

His phone buzzed. He saw it was PC Garrett calling. He answered it, all the time not taking his eyes off Kirsty.

'Yes, come on up, Garrett. It's all under control.'

He hung up.

'Right, shall we go into the kitchen?'

He reached into his overcoat pockets and produced two bottles of milk.

'Here we go, Mrs Byfield. Put the kettle on. I could murder a cuppa.'

....

Half an hour later, Drury and Garrett left the flat. They had not got very far. Kirsty Byfield knew her way around the police alright. She denied knowing anything about the Ice Squad's whereabouts. She did admit to having a brief fling with Gaz Lewis about a year ago, but that it had all fizzled out.

She told them that Liam Crooks was a lying little prick that had the hots for her, and when she rejected his advances, he became a complete pain. So she was not surprised that he had concocted this little tale of fantasy for the police to gain some sick revenge on her.

Drury had impressed upon her that it was a murder case they were investigating, and if she was hiding evidence or lying, then she was an accessory and would do prison time. For a moment, he had thought he detected a glimmer of fear in her eyes, but she was a hard-faced cow and soon regained her composure and said she knew nothing.

As both police officers got up to leave, Drury tried one more parting shot, telling Kirsty that she was on dangerous ground. If she knew anything about the murder and who did it, he told her, she was also a potential witness. The more witnesses to the crime, the more dangerous it could become, especially if the murderers thought the police were sniffing around pressing for a confession.

Kirsty Byfield said nothing. She just sat motionless at the kitchen table, with her arms tightly folded. The police officers saw themselves out and walked back to the car.

'She's lying. I can sense it,' said Drury.

Garrett nodded in agreement.

'So, what do you want to do?'

Drury pressed his key fob to unlock the car.

'I think we go back to the station and get another car from the carpool, as I am sure Kirsty has spotted this one, then we come back and wait and watch. I am confident she will lead us to the gang.'

'Okay, I'll phone the Gov and let him know,' replied Garrett.

From the balcony of the flats, Kirsty watched the blue Ford Mondeo drive away. She pulled her phone from her pocket and scrolled down in her address book until she found Gaz Lewis's number.

She texted him: *I need to see you asap x*

Tony Slade walked into the restaurant bar on Monday morning. He was in good spirits. The previous evening, he had gone to Cueva de los Verdes to a special acoustic concert by Canadian rocker Bryan Adams.

The venue was a series of breathtakingly beautiful caves, which were a major tourist attraction but also a well-known place for live music. Within the caves was a 500-seater auditorium. The unique surroundings and awesome acoustics made for a memorable experience.

He whistled *Summer of 69* as he helped himself to a black coffee from behind the counter.

Camilo and Lucy were in the kitchen and waved out to him.

'Morning, guys,' acknowledged Tony. 'Looks like another lovely day ahead.'

Camilo came into the bar, and Tony noticed a look of concern on his face.

'Are you okay, Camilo? Lucy and the baby alright?'

'Yes, boss, we are all fine, but I think you'd better have a look at this.'

He handed Tony a newspaper and walked away.

'Front page, and pages seven and eight,' he said, as he disappeared back into the kitchen.

Tony took the paper and picked up his coffee. He shouted after Camilo, 'What's the big news? Newcastle United deciding whether to sign Ronaldo or Messi?'

He frowned when Camilo did not answer.

Tony sat down at his favourite corner table and spread open the paper. It was *The Daily News*.

He scanned the cover and read the headline. He felt his blood run cold.

'Secret Love Child of Fugitive' stretched across the page, along with the standard grainy image of a young Tony Slade in his paratrooper days.

He read the front page and then turned to pages seven and eight, his hands trembling. He read about Ruby Carter, whose mother was Katy Carter née Connor.

Memories flooded back to him of his younger days and the relationship he had shared with Katy. They had both been young and in love, but his violent lifestyle of working on the doors had finished their relationship.

Tony had joined the parachute regiment and tried to forget the first girl he had ever loved. But a few years later, on leave back in Durham, he had run into her again. One thing had led to another and they had ended up in bed together. It had been a mistake. Katy was already in a relationship and going to emigrate to America with a Clint Carter.

Tony returned to the forces but, through the grapevine, had heard that Katy had given birth to a baby girl some months later. A small part of him had wondered if that had been the result of their one night of passion, but he had pushed the thought away. Their lives were going two completely different directions, and he could not offer Katy anything. Tony never heard anything from Katy to suggest he was the father of her child.

So, that had been it as far as Tony was concerned and he got on with his life. But every now and then, when he had lain awake at night in some Godforsaken war zone, he had turned over the idea that he might be a father.

And now here was the alleged evidence, all these years later, that he might just indeed have a daughter. A daughter named Ruby, who had apparently gone through the most terrible experience of her life by losing her father and then brother.

Her mother Katy was also in hospital. What a horrendous experience for her, and on top of this, Katy had decided to reveal a long-kept secret that Clint Carter had not been her biological father.

He carried on reading and discovered that the brother, Gary Carter, had been carrying a newspaper clipping of Tony Slade in his pocket when he died, and it was believed that he had been in the UK trying to find the man, at his sister's request. Ruby Carter was said to be in Bristol now to help police with their enquiries.

The article then went on to go over old news of Graig O Mor and the 'Coffee Shop Massacre' that had brought the name Tony Slade to prominence.

Although the police would still like him to come in for questioning, they had nothing but circumstantial evidence that he had committed any crimes at all.

He noticed that his old nemesis Steve Richmond, now DI Richmond, was heading up the murder investigation. *So, he had survived the fall from the cliff, after all. Fair play. Richmond was a resilient bastard.*

Tony closed the paper and sat back in his seat. His untouched coffee had long gone cold. He was sweating, although he was sitting under the cooling ceiling fan. His mind ran riot.

Katy Connor had been so long ago. He had really only been a boy. The paper stated that Ruby was thirty-eight years old and now running the *Manhattan News*. Like him, she had essentially lived her whole life not realising that he existed. *Why would she want to see him now? And what had happened to her brother Gary? Why was he pushed to his death?* Tony wondered. *Did it have anything to do with him?*

It was all too much to take in. Just when he'd thought that he had found a little bit of normality in his life after so much turmoil, something else just appeared to knock him down once again. This latest news had really floored him.

Tony looked at the article again and saw it was written by another name from his past: Susie Rawlings. It seemed too much of a coincidence that she had written this article, and that his old nemesis Richmond was heading the case.

He left the restaurant to concerned looks from Camilo and Lucy, but they knew better than to say anything. They guessed that he needed time and space to process the news he had just received.

Tony walked miles along the seafront, deep in his own thoughts. He could just throw the paper in the bin and forget about it all. He did not need to pursue the matter, but part of him wondered what Ruby looked like. Also, the soldier in him wanted to know why her brother had been pushed to his death, and what plan Rawlings and Richmond had cooked up for him.

By the time he returned to the restaurant, it was getting dark. He had come to a decision.

He could not stay here in Lanzarote. The people here would soon find out his true identity, and he did not want to bring trouble to Camilo and Lucy's doorstep. He had also decided he needed to speak to Ruby Carter face-to-face. It was risky going back, especially with Richmond sniffing around, but Tony had made his mind up. He was going to the UK to get to the bottom of this latest development in his life.

Tony Slade sat in a grey Vauxhall Astra across the road from Bridewell Police Station, keeping an eye on the comings and goings. He was sure that he would eventually see Ruby Carter.

He had taken the first flight out of Lanzarote he could get, and had arrived in Bristol on Monday evening. He had hired a car straight from the airport for the week, under the identity of Tony Swan, then booked into a Holiday Inn near the city centre. He hoped that this would give him enough time to sort things out.

Now, Tuesday morning, found him on surveillance – something he had been used to in the military.

Bridewell Police Station was the main station in Bristol, and he reckoned Ruby would be here at some point. He looked at an image of her taken from the internet. She had her mother's looks – same blue eyes and crooked smile. She was single and very career driven.

Katy had done well for herself in the States. A damn sight better than if she had stayed here. Tony would have been no father to Ruby. He was a restless spirit, always on the move. The army had been his family for so long, and he had never really found a replacement since he came out many years ago now.

His brief relationship with Annette had promised a new life, but it had been ripped away from him by his old life. With the news that he had a daughter who had tragically lost so much – including the man she had called her father – maybe, just maybe, he would be able to help her.

Tony was not sure how or even if she would want to see him, but he felt strangely compelled to meet her.

He felt uncharacteristically nervous. Tony Slade had faced more danger and adversity than he could remember and had always met it face-on. He had learned how to control and channel fear and make it work for him, but at this moment his stomach was in knots.

Handling a firefight or facing down an aggressive enemy was familiar territory for him, but this situation was well out of his comfort zone.

He sipped on his takeaway americano coffee, glanced again at the photograph, and waited.

Being back in Bristol felt strange. It had been a while, and the last time he had been here had not exactly been his finest hour. He had almost lost his life.

Tony could never have envisaged coming back again, but here he was. Putting himself in a precarious position yet again.

He studied the photo image of Ruby Carter once more, and wondered where this was all heading.

Four hours later, Tony was ready to call it a day. His back was stiff from sitting so long, and without a regular caffeine fix, he was finding his eyelids getting heavy.

He could think of no way to find Ruby other than staking out the police station. Apart from this location, he had no idea where she might be. He decided to give it another half an hour and then he would have to move on. He had been lucky to grab this space – one of the few without double yellow lines or parking restrictions on it. He was reluctant to give up without some success.

Just then, he saw DI Steve Richmond appear at the station entrance. He walked down the steps to the pavement and to a waiting car. Right behind him came a woman. Tony was in no doubt. It was Ruby Carter. At last, he had found her.

Ruby and Richmond got into the back seat of a Volvo V70. It pulled away from the curb and Tony headed straight after it. He kept a safe distance, and negotiated the traffic expertly to keep the Volvo in sight on the busy late afternoon roads in the centre of the city.

For a while after he came out of the forces, Tony had worked for a security firm in the North East that specialised in chauffeured bodyguard work for foreign diplomats visiting the UK. On many occasions, he had navigated tricky and extremely busy traffic, particularly when his work had brought him to London.

It had been well paid work, but short lived. It certainly had not been James Bond stuff, but he had picked up some extremely useful skills that he was once again putting into practice.

The Volvo finally came to a stop outside the Ravenscroft Hotel and Tony pulled in a little further down the road. He cautiously walked back and was just in time to see Richmond wave Ruby Carter goodbye at the hotel entrance. He waited until the Volvo pulled away then made his way towards the entrance just as she disappeared inside.

Ruby Carter entered the luxurious foyer of the Ravenscroft. The last few days had been a bit of a blur for her. The ordeal of seeing her brother and identifying his body had been the most traumatic experience of her life. The full realisation of losing two members of her family in quick succession had hit her hard. Then being shown the platform from where her brother had been pushed, had filled her heart with dread and sorrow.

DI Richmond had been so supportive to her, but she also knew that he had a job to do. Finally had come the questioning once more about Tony Slade. Ruby had gone over the same story she had given to Richmond previously. In return, he had provided her with more details on the 'Coffee Shop Massacre' and his adventure on the island of Graig O Mor in pursuit of Slade.

When he'd finished, Ruby had told Richmond that, on the evidence he had presented to her, she was not sure whether Tony Slade was a hero or a villain.

They had called it a day after that, and Ruby had asked to go back to her hotel.

Ruby walked to the main desk and asked the young man on duty if she had any messages. He informed her that she did not.

Ruby glanced at her wristwatch. The time read 5:30pm. She decided she needed a large vodka and cranberry juice, so she headed for the bar.

Tony entered the foyer and quickly scanned it. He immediately saw Ruby heading for the Oasis Bar, which luckily was also open to non-residents. He waited outside until he saw her order a drink and take a corner seat by the window that looked out onto the har-bourside.

He spied the bathrooms to his left of him, so he made for them. He suddenly felt nervous.

Inside the bathroom, he went to the huge mirror that ran the full length of the wall. Below the mirror sat a dozen sleek marble wash basins, all equipped with gold plated taps. Tony ran a tap and splashed a little cold water on his face then checked his appearance.

He had dressed casually, but smart, in a white cotton shirt and black jeans. Over the shirt, he wore a lightweight black leather jacket. He ran his eyes one last time over the mirror and then turned and left. This was the moment of truth.

When Tony entered the Oasis, there was only a handful of people occupying it. Most sat at their own tables engaged in conversations. Nobody took any notice of him as he walked over to the bar. A stunning red-haired girl was serving there. Her name badge informed Tony that her name was Bridget.

'What can I get you, sir?'

Her accent was pure Northern Irish. Tony had spent some years there in the 1970s, at the height of 'The Troubles'.

'A single Jack Daniels on the rocks, please,' he replied.

The girl gave him a winning smile.

'Coming right up. Do you want this charged on your room tab?'

'No, I'll pay it now, thanks.'

Bridget brought back the drink and Tony paid.

'Enjoy,' she said.

Tony raised his glass. 'Cheers, and thank you.'

He took a sip.

To be honest, he could have downed a double in the circumstances, but he was driving and did not want to attract any unwelcome attention from the police. He walked across to the table where Ruby sat. She was looking out of the window and was not yet aware of his presence.

'Mind if I join you, Ruby?'

Surprised at the mention of her name, Ruby looked up to see a man who, at first, she did not recognise.

He was middle-aged, ruggedly handsome, and seemed to be in good shape. *Was this guy trying to hit on her?* As nice as he seemed, she did not usually go for men of his age.

'I'm sorry. Do we know each other?' she said. 'You seem to have the advantage of knowing my name?'

'Hello, Ruby. Let me introduce myself. My name is Tony Slade and I believe you have been looking for me.'

Chapter ten

There was a moment of complete silence. It felt as though the whole room had just heard what had been said and was listening to the conversation.

At first, Tony saw fear flicker across her face. Then the fear seemed to change to resignation. Finally, she gestured with her hand towards a chair.

'Please. Please sit down. God, I don't know what to say. How did you find me? How did you know I was here in England? How did you recognise me?'

Tony sat down and placed his drink on the table.

'Which one of those questions would you like me to answer first?'

Ruby took a gulp of her drink but didn't reply.

'I'm sorry to shock you like this, Ruby, but I just couldn't contact you any other way. I only found out the other day through a British newspaper article that you exist and that I am your...' Tony hesitated.

'My dad,' finished Ruby.

Tony looked up into her ice blue eyes. 'Yes, your dad.'

It was his turn to take a drink. The bourbon tasted good.

'I read the terrible news about your family,' he continued. 'About the car crash, and then what happened to your brother. Apparently, he came over here looking for me. I can assure you his death had nothing to do with me. I no longer live in the UK.'

Ruby remained silent.

Tony went on, 'I knew your mum such a long time ago. I was just a boy finding my way in the world and your mum came into it, and for the short time I knew her, she made my life so special. At that time, I truly did love her.'

Ruby looked at the features of this man. She guessed from his background that it was not easy for him to bear his soul like this.

'My mum speaks fondly of you, too.'

'How is she?'

'She's getting a little stronger day by day, but it's going to be a long process.'

Tony nodded.

'Why do you think she decided to tell you this secret now? What did she think to gain from it?'

'I've thought long and hard about that,' Ruby told him, 'and the only gain she could get was to ease her conscience of a secret she has held onto for forty plus years. I think she thought that she was going to die. Mum married into a staunch Roman Catholic family. It must have riddled her with guilt to keep this secret, and with Dad… Clint… gone, I think she needed to unburden herself.'

'And how do you feel about it, Ruby?'

'As shellshocked as you, I guess, when I first found out. I felt my whole life was somehow fake, and the man I thought of as Dad… wasn't. He was a good man and a wonderful father and husband. He helped make me the person I am today. I loved him so much and I know Mum did. I miss him every day.

'For a while, I wished Mom hadn't told Gary and me about you. I just didn't need this new revelation in my life. Then, a little part of me wanted to know more about you. So, I dug around on the web and found some stuff. The only image I found of you was when you were in the parachute regiment. You were in your twenties. Apologies for not recognising you now.'

Tony held up his hand in a 'don't worry' gesture. A lot of water had gone under the bridge since then.

'I was never one for having my photo taken,' he admitted. 'Just as well it seems.'

Ruby continued, 'My brother Gary was also ex-military. He had been in the Marines. He seemed the ideal person to track you down and he was keen to do it for me. So, he went to England in search of you and... well, you know the rest.'

Tears came to Ruby's eyes. Tony wanted to reach out to comfort her, but he did not know what her reaction would be.

'I had to identify his body yesterday,' she said quietly. 'I was only allowed to see his face, as the rest of him was so badly messed up. I don't know what is happening to my fucking life. To cap it all off, I am sitting in a hotel bar talking to a stranger who is my father.'

Tony shifted awkwardly in his seat.

'Look, I'll leave if I'm making you uncomfortable. I'll give you some space.'

Ruby took a deep sigh and wiped her tears away.

'No, please stay. This situation is not your fault. You're right. It was me who was originally looking for you. I'm sorry for the outburst.'

Tony relaxed again.

'Look, Ruby. I'm sorry for what's happened. But, hand on heart, I had no idea that I had a daughter. Katy told me nothing whatsoever. She emigrated to the States and that was the last I heard of her, and that is the God's honest truth. I knew nothing of your family or their background. For the best part of my life, I have been in foreign countries, fighting in wars that had nothing to do with me. It's another life, far away from news and media.'

'Would it have made a difference to your life if you had known about me?' asked Ruby.

Tony drained his glass.

'To be honest, I don't know. I was a different person then to the one I am now. So, that's a question I can't answer. The only thing I know is that Katy chose not to tell me about you, and moved to the States to start her new life with Clint. Looking back on my track record, it was probably the right thing to do.'

Ruby was silent for a moment.

'Can I ask you something?' she said eventually.

'Sure. Fire away.'

'Are you a criminal?'

'Well, if you ask around enough, I expect you can find somebody who would tell you yes. I would prefer to say I have been a victim of circumstance.'

Ruby raised one carefully manicured eyebrow.

'Would you care to explain?'

Tony picked up her glass.

'Let me buy you another drink and I'll try to answer that question for you. One thing you should know, you have nothing to fear from me.'

Ruby smiled.

'Okay, I will have a vodka and cranberry juice, please.'

Ruby watched the man walk towards the bar. The whole situation was surreal. Two people meeting for the first time, having spent most of their adult life not knowing the other existed.

There was no blame to apportion here, except maybe to her mum. The question was, where did they go from here?

From an earlier conversation today with DI Richmond, he had made it obvious that he would love to speak with Tony Slade if he found his whereabouts, but that was not Ruby's concern. She had just found the man who was her real father, and there was something about him that told her she could trust him.

When Tony returned from the bar, she invited him to have dinner with her in the hotel restaurant.

Over a delicious meal of pulled pork in cider sauce, followed by raspberry and dark chocolate cheesecake, Tony told her about his past. He was surprised how easy it was to talk to her.

He told her how he had met her mum and the places they had gone on dates. He spoke about his early life in the North East, and living with his abusive and violent father. And he went on to recount his army career, and his later life working on the doors.

She, in turn, told him about her upbringing in New York, the success of the family newspaper business, and how she was now running it. She told him she had never married. Too selfish, maybe. She enjoyed her freedom too much and loved her job.

Ruby spoke about her mum and her dad. Then she told him more about her brother, and how he had drifted away from the family circle after leaving the Marines.

Tony could understand and appreciate this. He told Ruby that war changed a person forever, and as a result, they did not see the world as others do. It could be hard for a family to understand this.

They ordered coffee and took it to a couple of armchairs in the bar.

Tony took a sip of his black americano. He found it ironic that Ruby had ordered the same. Like father, like daughter.

He leaned over in his chair, towards Ruby.

'Look, Ruby. I need to ask you something. If Richmond asks if I have been in contact with you, say that you have heard nothing. The last thing I need while I am here is the police breathing down my neck.'

She regarded the serious features of this man with whom she felt so relaxed.

'Tony, I have no wish to get involved in a vendetta that this policeman has with you. I came to the UK to bring my brother back home. Me finding you wasn't on the agenda.'

She hesitated a moment as if she were trying to choose the right words.

'But now that we have met, I am glad. I hope we can salvage something from this terrible situation.'

Tony smiled. 'I do, too.'

'In that case, your secret is safe with me,' Ruby replied, 'Now, I want to ask *you* a favour.'

'Okay, I'm intrigued. What can I do for you?'

'Well, from what you have told me about yourself, I think you may just be the person to help me.'

'In what way?' asked Tony.

'Would you to help me find the men who killed my brother?' she answered.

Tony felt a tingle of adrenaline shoot through his body.

'I thought the police were doing that.'

Ruby explained to Tony what the police had unearthed so far about the flawed CCTV at the station, the Ice Squad and their leader, a Gaz Lewis, and how he was missing along with his mates. She also said they may be connected to a suspected drug dealer named Lenny Keating.

Ruby went on to tell Tony that, in the short time she had been here and co-operating with the police, they seemed to have drawn a blank. She also added that Richmond appeared to be more interested in finding him than her brother's killers. She needed that closure to resume her life and she just didn't have faith in the police.

Tony listened until she had told him all she knew.

'Look, Ruby. As I told you, I don't live in the UK any more, and my patch was the North East, not the South West. I wouldn't know where to start, so I'm not sure what I can do for you. I'm flattered that you think I can help.'

He saw the disappointment in her eyes, and she made to get up.

'Okay. Forget it, Tony. I shouldn't have asked you. I just thought with your military background and all...'

'Well, that didn't help your brother much, did it?'

Tony instantly regretted what he had said. He saw the hurt in Ruby's eyes and reached out and touched her hand.

'Wait, Ruby. I'm sorry. I shouldn't have said that. It was a cheap shot. I want to help you. I really do. You deserve that at least. Give me a day or so to get my bearings and see what I can do, okay?'

Ruby stared into his eyes.

'Please don't do this out of guilt for me. You owe me nothing, Tony. But I have nobody else to turn to that I can trust, and I don't want to go back to New York without finding Gary's killers and bringing them to justice.'

'Okay, Ruby. I will help you.'

They swapped phone numbers and Tony promised he would be in touch. It was getting late and they had spoken enough for one day.

Tony walked her to the lifts and bade her goodnight. He was surprised when she stepped forward and planted a soft kiss on his cheek.

'Things have been crazy lately and it seems as if I am just being swept along on a tidal wave. It is too early to know what relationship we will have, Tony. I am still getting around the fact that you exist. I guess only time will tell. For now, let's settle with we did okay tonight.'

With that, the lift arrived and she stepped into it and was gone.

Tony drove back to his accommodation deep in thought. Things had gone better than he could have hoped for tonight. In the short time he had known Ruby, she seemed to be a smart independent woman. A tough cookie. She reminded him so much of her mother.

After the tragic death of Annette, he had never thought he would open up to another woman like he had tonight.

Like Ruby, he had no idea where their relationship would go. He knew he certainly could not replace Clint and had no reason to want to do so. At sixty years of age, suddenly becoming a dad was not something that had been on Tony Slade's radar. And because of his violent past that seemed to have a habit of hurting anybody important to him, he really did not know how close he wanted Ruby to get.

He also knew that Richmond had been putting in the poison about him now that he had found out their secret. If the policeman knew that Ruby had met him tonight, he would be all over her, wanting to know where Tony was.

He had to agree with Ruby that Richmond was probably more concerned with using her to flush Tony out than trying to track down her brother's killers. Ruby would have to be careful. Richmond was a wily bastard.

What Tony did know was that he wanted to help Ruby. He felt he owed it to her. But at the same time, he knew that doing so would open up a whole nasty and dangerous can of worms, and he had to be ready to once more don the dark cloak of violence. Did he have any fight left in him? Sooner or later, he felt he was about to find out.

As he pulled into the Holiday Inn car park, he realised he had more questions than answers at the moment.

Kirsty Byfield made her way along the dockside. It was midnight and the place was deserted. The moon cast an eerie slivery glow over the water where numerous sized boats and barges were moored.

The dockside had a warren of pathways leading off it, which could be quite disorientating, but Kirsty knew her way around well. She had been here many times before under the cover of darkness.

Earlier that day, Gaz Lewis had returned her text and told her to come and meet him tonight, but to be careful. She promised him that she would.

She also came bearing gifts – three family bags of Nacho Cheese Doritos, and a bottle of vodka and one of scotch. Kirsty fancied a little party. It would all be good, especially if Gaz had some skunk on him.

She had clocked the unmarked police car back at the flats. It was a different one to earlier, but she knew it was them. She had waited until dark and then sneaked down the fire escape then weaved her way behind the large industrial waste bins to exit the flats the back way. Easy when you knew how. The two coppers sat in their car were oblivious to the fact. *Idiots*. This was her patch, and she knew it inside out. She had been street-wise since she had been old enough to play outside. The cops were no match for her.

She now followed a dimly lit alleyway. At the far end stood the warehouse she was looking for. Back in Bristol's heyday of shipping, this warehouse, like many others, had stored tea, coffee, grain or tobacco. Since then, it had been used as a boat repair yard for a while, but now it was just a large empty hulking space whose only inhabitants were the water's rats and a few homeless people.

Kirsty picked up her pace. Every now and then, she glanced over her shoulder just to make sure that she was not being followed. Finally, she reached the warehouse and walked around the corner to a small shuttered side door. She rapped on it with the special code she and Gaz shared. A minute later, the door opened, and a torch beam appeared. Kirsty slipped inside and the door was shut and bolted tight.

In the torchlight, she could make out the features of Gaz. They looked gaunt and ghostly.

'Hi, babe. You alright?' she asked.

Gaz ignored the question.

'What did you bring?' He eyed the bag in her arms.

'Booze and snacks, as promised,' replied Kirsty.

'Right, follow me and watch your step. There's all sorts of crap lying on the floor.'

Kirsty followed Gaz and the pale light of his torch until they entered a small room that was lit by half a dozen camping lamps. There was a couple of makeshift beds on the floor. Ethan Riggs was sprawled out asleep on one of them.

Apart from that, the room was pretty much bare, except for a small battered wooden table and two chairs. On the table were the remains of a KFC meal and a dozen empty beer cans.

'Fucking hell, Gaz. You look like shit. What the hell is going on?'

'Thanks, Kirsty. You don't exactly look like Taylor Swift yourself.'

Kirsty huffed and began to get out the drinks and snacks. Gaz seemed to lighten up a little.

'Great! I am fucking starving!'

He ripped open a bag of Doritos and stuffed a handful of the chips into his mouth. The rustling of the bag woke Ethan who yawned and sat up.

'Alright, Kirsty. I didn't hear you come in. Is that food you got there?'

He jumped to his feet and joined Gaz at the table. Kirsty watched them both eating hungrily like animals.

'What the fuck is all this? Why are you hiding in here?'

Gaz took a long swig from the bottle of scotch and coughed loudly as the amber fluid burned its way down to his belly.

'We aren't hiding. We just needed to take the heat off for a few days. That's all.'

'Then why have the police been around my mum's asking me questions?'

Gaz glanced nervously at Ethan.

'The police have been around? What the fuck did they want?'

Kirsty twisted open the top on the bottle of vodka and took a sip.

'They wanted to know if I knew where you, Ethan, and Harvey were, as you seemed to have disappeared from your patch without a trace.'

'And what did you say?' asked Gaz.

'Fuck, Gaz. I said nothing. I told them I didn't know where you were.'

Gaz took another drink.

'Right. Good. You're sure you weren't followed here?'

Kirsty rolled her eyes. 'Of course not. I'm not stupid. Jesus.'

This seemed to momentarily satisfy Gaz.

Kirsty continued, 'The police mentioned the murder of that dude on the railway station. They seem to think you guys had something to do with it. Did you?'

Gaz moved quickly across the table and grabbed Kirsty by the face, pinching her cheeks tightly until her eyes watered. He came up so close that she could smell the whisky and cheese on his breath. She could see a wild and haunted look in his eyes that she had not seen before. It frightened her.

'That is nothing to do with you. Understand? Keep your nose out and your mouth shut.'

Ethan spoke up.

'Okay, Gaz. Take it easy, mate.'

Gaz let go and pushed her away.

Kirsty rubbed her face. 'Fuck, Gaz. That hurt. There was no need for that. I won't say anything. I promise.'

Gaz went back to the bottle.

'Where's Harvey?' asked Kirsty.

Gaz glared back at her. Ethan spoke again.

'He went to visit his brother in Manchester. He's ill or something.'

Kirsty sensed Ethan was lying. She couldn't recall Harvey ever mentioning he had a brother, but she decided not to push things when Gaz was in such a foul mood.

'How long do you plan to stay here? Not only have the police been asking for you, but apparently, according to that dick Robbie Spencer, Lenny Keating has also been looking. He's left Spencer in charge of the Ice Squad's patch in your absence.'

Kirsty saw fear flicker in the boys' eyes before Gaz regained his composure.

'Right. Well, we'll be back in a few days. Like I say, just needed to cool a few things. That's all. No big deal.'

'Okay, Gaz. Just be careful with the police sniffing around. I'm sure they'll be back again. Plus, Robbie Spencer isn't the sharpest tool in the box to leave in charge of business.'

Gaz laughed.

'Yeah. Okay, babe. Look, I'm sorry about a minute ago. I'm just a bit wired, that's all. Come here. I got a bit of good stuff under the mattress. Let's have a smoke and chill for a bit, yeah?'

When Kirsty Byfield finally left a few hours later, Gaz sat down with Ethan.

'Look, man. It's time to get the fuck out of Bristol for good, but back at my flat is a hardcore stash of weed. It's worth some good coin on the streets. Also, there's money owed to Keating that I have. Well, fuck him. Now that's ours. We need to get back there and get it before we go. We can't ever come back to Bristol. Not now that Lenny has killed Harvey and the police are sniffing around.

'If they put the heat on Keating, he's going to offer us up as the sacrificial lambs to save his own fucking murdering black ass. If he has us back working for him, we're just going to be his two little bitches, always looking over our shoulder. Any clout we had in the neighbourhood will be gone. We will lose credibility, and in the drug business, that spells death. Any way you look at it, we are fucking screwed. So, I suggest we go back, get the gear, and go to pastures new. Agreed?'

Ethan nodded.

'Okay, Gaz. When?'

'I bet that prick Robbie Spencer will be on the lookout for us and report straight to Keating. Can you believe Keating putting that muppet in charge? He couldn't manage his own shit into the pan, let alone our business,' chuckled Gaz.

He looked across to Ethan.

'It will be dangerous, but it's our last chance to get out of here with something. So, it's worth the risk. We'll go tomorrow.'

*

In the shadows of the darkened buildings, Luke Drury watched Kirsty Byfield leave the warehouse. She was a clever little bitch, but not clever enough. He had left Garrett in the car and followed Byfield on foot. The gamble of waiting at the rear of the flats had paid off. He now knew where the Ice Squad boys were holed up. He had nailed them.

He reached for his phone but then decided against it. It was late. This information could wait for now.

He smiled to himself as he returned the phone to his pocket and began walking back to his car.

Chapter eleven

The next morning, Tony was up early. He pushed out fifty press-ups, then showered and made a cup of hot black coffee from the facilities provided in the room.

He sat on a chair by a small desk in front of a window that overlooked the car park. He picked up his mobile from the desktop. He had a burner phone that could not be detected, and he had been using one since he left Graig O Mor. Although he was now living under the new identity of Tony Swan, he still did not trust modern technology, and worried that somehow he could be traced.

He had to make a few phone calls and he was not looking forward to the first one.

Tony called the number, and after half a dozen rings, a gruff Geordie voice answered.

'Who is this? You better have a good fucking reason for waking me up at this time.'

'Morning, Joe. This is Tony Slade.'

There was a moment's silence and then the gruff voice sounded again.

'Well, fuck me. And to what do I owe the pleasure of this early morning wake-up call from you then?'

Joe Walsh was a face from the past. Ironically, he had saved Tony's life on the island of Graig O Mor when Tony had thought that he had come to kill him.

Joe, along with Danny Ewan, had taken over the criminal empire of the deceased Kenny Robbins in the North East. Their history went way back. The last time they had spoken, Tony had been suffering from the onset of hypothermia after being dragged out the Bristol Channel and into a helicopter. Walsh had saved his life, but with the stipulation never to come back to the North East. It was a deal which Tony had stuck to, but now he needed the man's help once again.

'I need to pick your brains, Joe,' answered Tony.

A chuckle came back down the phone to him.

'You have got some neck, Slade, I'll give you that. I thought the deal when I saved your sorry ass was that we parted company for good?'

'Look, Joe. I've stayed away from Newcastle and I have no intention of ever returning. I will keep my word. I just need to ask you a few questions. How can that hurt?'

'Maybe I don't want to talk to you, Slade. Did that ever occur to you?'

'Please, Joe. Just a few minutes.'

There was silence again. Then Joe spoke.

'You have two minutes, so don't fucking waste them.'

Tony sighed with relief.

'Have you ever heard of a guy in the South West in your type of business, named Lenny Keating?'

'What the fuck do you want with that screwball? What have you got into now, Slade?' replied Joe Walsh.

'You don't want to know, Joe. Believe me. Well, I take it you know him.'

'Yeah. I know of his reputation. He is some big name in Bristol, I believe. Got a big black finger in many illegal pies. I hear he is a dangerous fucker. I would stay well clear.'

'I'll bear that in mind. Also, what about the Ice Squad?'

'Never heard of them. Are they a new boyband?'

Tony laughed.

'No, I think they are connected to Keating in some way.'

'Well, with a name like that, if they aren't a fucking pop group, then I would imagine they are some wannabe gangster gang. They're probably drug mules for Keating.'

'Okay. Thanks, Joe. I owe you.'

'Fuck off, Slade, and don't ring me again.'

The phone went dead.

Well, that confirmed what the police thought.

Tony called Ruby's number and asked her what area of Bristol this Ice Squad hung out in. She told him what Richmond had told her. He thanked her and promised to call again later.

Finally, he phoned his friend, Brian James, in Morocco. He explained his situation and asked him if he had a military contact in the South West. Tony had lost a good friend and ex-army buddy, Doug Jacobs, who had been Mr Fixit for him if he needed anything of an unconventional nature. He was now out of the network, but Brian told him to leave it with him a day or so.

Lenny Keating sat at his desk in the office of *Roxy's*. His morning ritual was to get up at 6am and workout at the gym. Then he'd have breakfast in a small Italian café/bar called *Dino's*. After that, it was back to one of his clubs to read through the news headlines on the internet and then get on with business.

He scanned the headlines, half concentrating, until something caught his eye. He came across a news story that immediately stopped his random scrolling. He read about the death of Gary Carter – the man Banks had shoved to his death – and how the police were tracking down some solid leads.

This was not what unduly worried him, but what did give him concern was that this Gary Carter had been the son of the deceased millionaire newspaper owner Clint Carter. That changed things totally.

Gary Carter had not just been some faceless drifter; he had been the son of one of the most powerful businessmen in the world. A businessman who had also been a massive anti-drugs campaigner.

The article also revealed that Carter's daughter, and now head of the *Manhattan News*, was coming to the UK to help police with their enquiries.

Keating knew that, with this high-profile American connection, the UK police would be under extreme pressure to search high and low for the killers. There would be no stone left unturned. Fucking hell, even the President had stuck his ten cents' worth in. This was now going to become a big newsworthy case. He knew the police would be paying him a visit sooner rather than later, and he needed to be ready.

That wanker Banks had certainly chosen the wrong victim. He needed to find Lewis and Riggs and put them out of the picture before they spilled their cowardly guts.

But one thing in his favour was Ruby Carter. This woman had just become a valuable commodity to him. Maybe there was a way out of this mess if he used her as a hostage. At this moment, she was of more value alive than dead. He grabbed his phone and hit speed dial. It connected after half a dozen rings.

'Have you any updates for me?'

Keating listened to the reply and then growled down the phone.

'You better get something asap.'

He promptly hung up, then bellowed from the office, 'Joel, get the fuck in here now. We need to sort something fast.'

Gaz Lewis and Ethan Riggs stood in the shadows of the large wrought iron gates at the entrance to Bridge Park. This was their playground for business. They watched Robbie Spencer strutting around like the Cock of the North. A small group of youngsters on bikes congregated around him, hoping to be put to work.

'Look at that prick thinking he is the main man. He is nothing; just Keating's fucking puppet,' said Gaz Lewis.

'Look. Fuck him, Gaz. Let's just get to your gaff, get the goods, and go. I am fucking nervous being out here. You never know where any of Keating's boys are lurking.'

'Yeah, I suppose you're right, but I would still like to smash that twat right up.'

'Forget it, Gaz. We are done here. Let's just get the fuck away from this place.'

Gaz Lewis had never liked or trusted Robbie Spencer. Since he had been part of the gang, he felt that Spencer had resented his leadership and wanted his job. He was always ass-licking around Keating. Gaz knew Spencer had been posted here today to specially keep an eye out for him and report in.

Lewis heard his phone ping. It was a text from Kirsty. He had contacted her earlier and asked her to check on his house, and to tell him if anybody was hanging around. Her text just confirmed that the coast was clear.

'Right, that was Kirsty, and it's safe to go to my house. Let's do it.'

Gaz took one more glance in Robbie Spencer's direction, and it was exactly at that moment that the boy looked in the direction of the gates and they made eye contact. Spencer instantly recognised Lewis and Riggs.

Lewis made a gun shape with his finger and thumb and pointed it in his direction. Spencer immediately picked up his disregarded bike and pedalled off fast.

'Shit, Gaz. Now what?' asked Riggs.

Gaz Lewis laughed.

'Now, nothing. Let's go get the stash. We will be far away by the time he gets his scrawny ass to Keating.'

Kirsty Byfield sat in her mum's red Ford Corsa across the road from Gaz Lewis's house. She had taken the keys whilst Elsie Byfield was engrossed in 'Lorraine' on the television.

She had brought the car on the understanding that Gaz was going to take her with him when he left. The car would be a perfect getaway. Her mum did not drive it every day, so she would not know it was gone until she finally wandered down to the car park to find it missing. By then, they would be far away.

She kept watch up and down the street, then glanced over at 5 Gerrish Terrace – a rundown Victorian terraced house that had probably not seen a lick of paint since the Queen's Silver Jubilee. Gaz lived there on and off with his useless alcoholic dad, Fred, who was a complete waste of space. There was no sign of him, so Kirsty presumed he was still sleeping off last night's booze.

Gaz lived between here with his old man and 20 Doe Place, a few miles away, with his mum Shelley, whenever the mood took him. His parents had split some years ago and hated each other's guts. Gaz was not particularly fond of either of them as they had made his childhood a nightmare, but both provided somewhere to rest his head now and again, so Gaz flitted from both properties as and when.

Kirsty spied Gaz and Ethan walking down the street, looking furtively around them like frightened sheep. Whatever Gaz had got himself into, it must be bad for him to act like this.

She suspected that he did have something to do with the murder at the railway station, but she didn't care. She worshipped him, and would do whatever he asked. She had no life or future here, so she was prepared to go wherever Gaz wanted.

Joel Sterling and Big Will sat in the Range Rover watching the house.

Thirty minutes previously, as Joel was listening to Keating's update him on the latest turn of events, Keating had received a phone call from Robbie Spencer telling him that he had just spotted Lewis and Riggs at Bridge Park. He surmised that they were probably heading back to Gaz's house.

As soon as Joel was told, he was straight on it. They had come here a few times in the last few days, but without luck. They hoped now that third time would be lucky.

'You think the twat will actually come here, Joel?' asked Big Will.

'If he has money or a stash here, then yes, he will. He'll need it if he's planning to run. Just sit tight and we'll have the pair of bastards.'

Both men checked the guns they had concealed under their coats.

Gaz spotted the car and Kirsty sitting in the driver's seat. Sweet, she had done the job. He went up to the open driver's side window, leaned in, and planted a kiss on her lips.

'Good girl. Any problems?' he asked.

Kirsty shook her head.

'Right, I'm going into the house. I'll be five minutes, then I will be back. Ethan, mate, get in the car with Kirsty and drive down to the corner of the road and wait for me. Text me if you see anybody snooping about.'

Gaz Lewis crossed the road and let himself into the house. All was quiet. The place smelled of stale sweat, takeaways, and booze. As he made his way up the stairs, he noticed discarded clothes on the stairs.

He passed his father's bedroom. The door was ajar, and he saw the man crashed out on top of the bed, snoring like a pig. He was naked, and so was the bleach-bottled blonde lying next to him. An empty vodka bottle was hanging from his father's fingertips.

Gaz moved into his own bedroom, went to the wardrobe, and opened it. He knelt down and removed a few pairs of trainers in cardboard boxes from the bottom. Both still had the price tags on them.

He then removed a wooden panel from the floor and revealed a hiding space. He reached in and pulled out four large bundles of notes wrapped in elastic bands. This was followed by two plastic bags of weed. He grabbed a holdall and shoved the stuff into it.

Gaz then went back to the space and reached in again. This time, he fished out a Browning automatic and a spare clip. Gaz had purchased the gun from Ronnie Patterson a while back as a bit of extra protection. He had never used it to date.

He checked the gun, shoved it into the front of his waistband, and zipped up his jacket. He threw the clip into the bag and glanced around the room. There was nothing else of value.

On the way out, he caught sight of a small framed photo on the bedside table. It showed two young boys sitting on a beach somewhere. One was slightly older than the other. Both were smiling as they ate their ice cream cones.

Gaz and his younger brother Mark, way back in happier days. Mark had died of meningitis, aged five, and Gaz had never got over it. His brother had been the only light in an otherwise bleak world. He picked up the photo frame and dropped it into the holdall.

He ran back down the stairs and out of the front door. He checked up and down the street. It seemed clear. He broke into a sprint until he reached the car.

Kirsty and Ethan saw him coming. Gaz ran around to the driver's side and opened the door. He knew what he had to do.

'Did you get it, Gaz?' asked Ethan.

Gaz's eyes glazed over as he pulled the gun from his waistband.

'Right, both of you get the fuck out of the car. NOW.'

Both Kirsty and Ethan were initially shocked, and then frightened.

'Gaz, what the fuck are you doing?' exclaimed Kirsty.

Gaz thrust the gun into her face.

'Both of you get out of the fucking car.'

They both stumbled out.

'Gaz, I don't understand. Why?' asked Ethan.

'Because I have a better chance of surviving on my own than having to carrying you two as well. Sorry, but that's the way it is. I'm fed up with working with muppets. That prick Banks has spoiled it for all of us. I need to get away and start afresh. On my own. I have always managed on my own. Now move away from the car.'

As Gaz went to get into the car, Kirsty made a grab for the gun.

'No. Please don't, Gaz.'

Gaz pulled the gun away and it just went off.

Kirsty was thrown back six feet by the close retort. Blood gushed from the wound in her abdomen. There was an exit hole in her back the size of an adult's fist. She sat on the pavement in an upright position. Her eyes first full of surprise and then realisation, she tried to speak, but no words came out. She died in front of the boy she loved.

Gaz froze in shock. He just stood there staring at her. Ethan broke the silence.

'Fucking hell. What have you done? What the fuck have you done?'

Gaz glanced at Ethan. Something for a moment passed between them, and then Gaz jumped in the car and sped off. Ethan looked around in panic. An old man across the road had come out of his house to see what all the noise was about. Others were following suit.

Ethan took one last glance at the dead body of Kirsty and then broke into a run.

Both men were growing restless. How long would they have to be here, and where was Lewis?

Joel called up Lenny Keating to tell him all was quiet. Keating said he would speak to Spencer again and get back. A few minutes later, he rang back. There was urgency in his voice.

'Right. Listen up. I just questioned Spencer about the address you're at. That is Lewis's mum's house. 'Einstein' has now remembered that Lewis also occasionally dosses down at his dad's. That is probably where he headed. Address 5 Gerrish Terrace. Get on it. We can't afford to lose him now.'

As the phone call ended, Joel Sterling was already on his way.

Ethan Riggs ran blindly. Tears stung his eyes. He could not believe what had just happened. He did not have a clue where he was going, but he knew that he had to put some distance between himself and the crime scene. He had thought he and Gaz were mates, brothers even. And then there was Kirsty. Christ, she was dead. Poor Kirsty, who never hurt a fly.

Suddenly, he saw a black Range Rover bearing down on him. It ground to a halt in a skid of rubber and Big Will jumped out, scooped Riggs up like a rag doll, and threw him into the back seat.

The vehicle moved off again.

Joel Sterling looked in the rear-view mirror at the cowering figure of Riggs.

'Where is Lewis? I warn you, do not fucking lie to me.'

Ethan spilled his guts to the men. He no longer had a reason to support Gaz.

They took in the information without a flicker of emotion, then headed off in the direction Ethan Riggs had given them, looking for a red Corsa.

Chapter twelve

DI Steve Richmond hung up the call and threw his phone onto the desk. He had just spoken to Ruby Carter about finalising the details to have her brother's body flown home to the States. He had also asked if anybody had been in contact with her. She replied that they had not.

He knew the newspaper article had been a gamble, but in his gut he still believed Slade would show. In the time he had known him, Richmond knew that Slade had a sense of right and wrong, although he sailed close to the breeze at times.

At the funeral of his late Governor DCI Wyatt, there had been a large wreath of lilies sent to the crematorium with Slade's name on it. The bastard did have a conscience, and that was why Richmond sensed Slade would come looking for the daughter he had never known existed. Maybe he already had?

Suddenly, his phone rang. He picked it up. It was Sergeant Luke Drury calling.

'Gov, there's been a report of a gunshot on Gerrish Terrace, Southfield. One person down. A female. There was a report of two young men and a girl arguing outside a red Corsa about half hour ago.'

'Do you think this is our boys?'

'Yes, Gov. I think we have got a break. I am on my way there right now. ETA, five minutes.'

'Okay, Luke. I'm on my way.'

'The female shot was Kirsty Byfield, Gov. She died instantly. From the description of a neighbour, it looks like the shooter was certainly Gaz Lewis. The other guy is probably Riggs.'

They stood at the crime scene on Gerrish Terrace, which had been cordoned off. The paramedics were just covering the body of Kirsty Byfield in preparation to remove it to the morgue. SOCO had finished with her.

'The neighbour, a Mr Harold Harper, said one man jumped into the car and sped off whilst the other one ran off up the road.'

Sergeant Drury closed the notebook he had been reading from.

'What a fucking mess,' said Richmond. 'How come we didn't check out this address before, Luke?'

Drury looked embarrassed.

'That's what I was on my way to do, Gov. It wasn't easy finding any fixed abode for these guys. They aren't exactly home birds.

Richmond grunted in response, then asked, 'Any ID on the car or the man who ran off yet?'

'No, not yet Gov.'

PC Debbie Garrett stepped up and whispered in Drury's ear. He nodded in acknowledgement.

'We have just received a report of a stolen red Corsa. Owner Elsie Byfield.'

Richmond chewed over the information as he surveyed the crime scene.

'It looks like Lewis and Riggs were planning to leave Bristol with the help of Kirsty Byfield, and something went drastically wrong here. It was definitely just two men?'

Drury nodded.

'Well, if they were Lewis and Riggs, where the hell was Harvey Banks? Apparently, the three of them are joined at the hip.'

His question was met by silence.

The bearlike bulk of forensic pathologist Terry Hutchins came towards both policemen.

'Hello, Steve,' he said.

'What have you got, Terry?' asked Richmond.

'The victim died almost immediately. One bullet from what initially looks like a Browning. The bullet tore through her abdominal aorta. She didn't suffer. I will know more when we get her back to the lab.'

Richmond nodded.

'Thanks.'

He waited for the man to walk away.

'Right, Luke. Let's crack on and find this car."

Richmond's phone rang. He checked the caller ID and cursed under his breath. It was Chief Superintendent Hardwick.

'I am going to have to take this, Luke. Get on it, okay?'

Drury was still shocked at the death of the Byfield girl. She had not been a criminal as such; she had just got involved with the wrong people. She had not deserved to end up this way.

She had somehow cleverly stolen the car in an effort to aid and abet Lewis, and now she was dead. Drury could not help but feel partly responsible. He should have pulled her in the night he had followed her to the warehouse. He had failed to do so, but he'd had his own reasons for letting her go. Now it was too late. She was collateral damage.

The Range Rover picked up speed as it hit the dual carriageway. Joel's eyes watched every car, scanning to see the red Corsa, while Big Will watched Ethan Riggs. He had a gun trained on the boy, but Riggs hardly registered it. He seemed to have gone into shock and sat there motionless.

'That bastard has got to be on here. This is the only way to join the motorway. He couldn't have gone anywhere else,' said Joel.

Then he saw the car. It was on the hard shoulder, and Lewis was standing looking at a flat driver's side front tyre.

Joel smiled. *The Lord works in mysterious ways indeed*. As he indicated and pulled in behind the Corsa, Lewis saw him, and recognition registered on his face. The boy broke into a sprint, jumped the crash barrier, and disappeared into the undergrowth beyond.

Joel jumped out of the driver's seat of the Range Rover and ran in hot pursuit of the fleeing Lewis, but not before shouting back, 'Will, follow me and bring our passenger.'

He then disappeared into the undergrowth.

Gaz Lewis ran blindly through the wooded area. He had no idea where he was going, plus he had left the bag of money and drugs back in the car. He was fucked.

He could hear crashing in the undergrowth behind him, but his fear gave him an extra burst of energy.

Up ahead, he saw a clearing and a high wire fence which seemed to surround a large group of industrial units. Hope rose in his heart. If he could clear the fence, he might just get away.

He stopped to catch his breath and glanced back over his shoulder. Nobody was visible.

Gaz drew one more deep breath and broke into a sprint, ready to hit the fence. Unfortunately for him, in the long grass before the fence was some fly-tipped rubbish and he went ploughing through empty paint tins, bricks, and bin bags full of smashed-up plaster and masonry. He tripped spectacularly, spraining his left ankle.

He cried out in agony and rolled over on his back, pain shooting up his leg. He tried to stand, but fell again. And then, a shadow loomed over him. He looked up to see Joel Sterling standing there pointing a gun with a huge suppressor on it into his face. Next, Big Will lumbered into view. He had a gun, with the same type of suppressor on it, pointed into Ethan Riggs' back.

'Well, isn't this nice to all meet up again?' said Joel. 'You have certainly been giving us the runaround, boys. Lenny is well pissed. Anyway, all's well that ends well. Now, stay where you are, Gaz. I just need to give Lenny a call and see what he wants to do.'

Without taking his eyes off Gaz, he fished his phone out of his pocket and hit speed dial.

'Lenny, we have them both. Tracked them down to some woods off the dual carriageway. Do you want me to bring them back or what?'

Joel listened as he was given instructions. Finally, he nodded and said, 'Understood.'

He pocketed the phone.

'Well, there's good news and bad news. The good news is Lenny doesn't want to see you. The bad news is he wants business settled here and now.'

Gaz scrambled to a seated position.

'Shit, Joel. There's no need for this. Harvey is dead. He was the one who pushed that bloke. Why are Ethan and I answerable as well?'

'Because the police are sniffing, and Lenny doesn't trust you not to sell his ass out to save your own skins, so you've got to go. The man that Banks pushed has high power connections. The fucking heat is coming down on us all because of you clowns.'

Gaz squirmed on the grass. He desperately wanted to make a run for it, but he knew it was useless.

'Joel, man, look at Ethan. He's done. He isn't going to be a problem. Look at him. He is broke.'

Joel glanced towards Ethan and Big Will. That was the moment Gaz Lewis needed to unzip his jacket and reach for the Browning in his waistband.

As Joel turned back, Gaz Lewis had pulled the gun free and was levelling it. This surprised Joel, but Lewis was an amateur and took too long to pull the trigger. Joel managed to fire his gun first. The bullet hit Lewis between the eyes, blowing the back of his head off. He was dead before he fell back on the grass.

Big Will pushed Ethan Riggs forward, face down into the grass. The boy did not attempt to struggle as the big man fired two shots into his back and one in his head.

Joel picked up the Browning automatic from the grass and looked at Will.

'Can you believe that, bro? The cheeky bastard had a gun. Fucking hell.'

He looked down at the dead body of Gaz Lewis and put two more bullets in him.

'Right, Will. Let's go.'

The two men came out onto the dual carriageway. The plan had been for Will to drive the Corsa away and torch it, but they saw a police car cruising down the opposite side of the carriageway. So, they decided to forget that idea and get the hell out of there before the law hit the roundabout and came back up the other side.

An hour later, DI Steve Richmond got a call from PC Debbie Garrett informing him that a motorist had reported an abandoned red Corsa on the Dunster Green dual carriageway just outside Southfield. In the passenger seat of the car, the police had found a holdall containing £50,000 in cash and about £25,000 worth of weed.

Garrett went on to drop the bombshell that the two policemen on the scene had searched the woods beyond the hard shoulder, and discovered two bodies. Early indication showed that it was Gaz Lewis and Ethan Riggs of the Ice Squad gang. They had been brutally executed. There were all the hallmarks of a gang hit. The witness had also seen a black Range Rover drive away from the scene and taken a photo of it. Garrett finished by saying that she had sent the image over to the crime lab technicians to see if they could enhance it and get a number plate reading.

'Good work, Garrett. With those two murdered and Harvey Banks missing, I guess somebody got to them before we could. And seeing they supposedly worked for Lenny Keating, what are the bets that the black Range Rover belongs to him? Let me know as soon as you hear anything from the lab guys, okay?'

Garrett assured her boss that she would.

Richmond sat back in his office chair and clasped his hands behind his head. He could not keep a smug grin off his face. This was the perfect break he needed. After 'Hard Dick' had chewed his ass off earlier for lack of progress, he was going to take great pleasure in unloading this latest news on him. However, he wanted to hang fire to see if he could deliver the golden egg of the Range Rover belonging to Keating.

Delivering Keating's head on a plate, and not just these small cogs in the wheel, would be a triumph. There might even be a commendation in it for him. This day was beginning to turn out better than he'd thought. Now all he needed was that bastard Slade to surface somewhere and he would have the full house.

Richmond decided to call Ruby Carter and put her in the picture that, to all intents and purposes, her brother's killers had been brought to justice, but not in the way he had intended. If Keating was behind these executions, then he would nail his ass.

As his ex-Governor John Wyatt used to say, 'I can't have killing on my patch. I am in charge, not them.'

Keating had been plying his illegal drug trade for long enough and getting away with it, but this time Richmond might just be able to have him bang to rights for murder.

Richmond spoke with Ruby and explained the latest developments. He told her that he was sorry he had not been able to bring her brother's killers to justice, but he was now on the case to prosecute Lenny Keating, the big man behind the employment of the likes of Harvey Banks, Gaz Lewis, and Ethan Riggs. The trio had been lost and vulnerable kids looking for a way out of their non- existent lives. Looking for acceptance and worth, even if it meant running drugs for scum like Keating – a man who did not give a shit about them. He just saw them as commodities to use as and when. Keating knew that the lure of money was all it took. But when the time arrived, these kids were expendable, as recent events had proved.

Although Keating had not pushed her brother, Richmond believed he was ultimately responsible. The man thought he was above the law, and now it had to stop.

Ruby asked him what the chances were of making any charges stick against Keating. Richmond replied that they would do their best to get the evidence they needed to develop a water-tight case. Ruby told him that she could stay a month in the UK on her passport, and asked to be updated regularly.

Richmond finished the call by asking if Tony Slade had been in contact as yet, and again she said no. He began to wonder if Slade had taken the bait in the first place, or if perhaps Ruby was lying to him?

Tony Slade had received a phone call from Ruby Carter, informing him of her latest phone conversation with Richmond.

'So, justice has been done in a roundabout way, Ruby.'

'Yes, I suppose it has. I came here wanting those boys' blood, I truly did,' she admitted, 'but now finding out how this Lenny Keating used and manipulated them, I almost feel sorry for them. How fucking crazy is that?'

'I understand how you feel. In the army, I had the same feelings. When you went to war against a fellow soldier, you knew deep down that they were being manipulated, just as I was, by a higher power who would never dirty their own hands. I've had many a sleepless night over what I did, in the name of war. There are lots of people at the top of the tree who have the blood of thousands on their hands, yet they sleep like babies at night.'

'This Keating is a bad man, Tony. He exploits the young and vulnerable. He uses them for his nefarious activities and then just disposes of them like garbage. It's not right. He's inadvertently the root cause of Gary's death.'

'I understand how you feel, but taking on a man like Keating and his firm is dangerous, Ruby. They are major league, not a bunch of wayward kids,' replied Tony.

'I do know that. I am not naïve, Tony, nor am I some shrinking violet. My newspaper prints news about the real world. I know how it works. I'm a big girl.'

Tony could detect the irritation in her voice and tried to smooth the waters.

'I know you are, Ruby, but I am concerned you may be taking on something bigger than you realise.'

'Look, Tony. You must understand, my father... I mean, Clint Carter.' She coughed awkwardly.

'Hell, anyway, the man worked tirelessly with the mayor and the chief of the NYPD to help expose and shut down numerous drug dealers and their businesses. Our newspaper can be an enormously powerful voice, even across the Atlantic. I have many contacts, and I could help put this man behind bars forever. I have the finance and influence, through my paper, to make a difference. To take a personal tragedy and turn it around for the good of many. I owe it to my brother's memory.'

Tony did not like where this conversation was going. He sensed that he was on a loser by trying to convince this strong-minded young woman not to go forward with her plans, but he had to have one more try.

'Ruby, I hear you, but from what Richmond has said, Keating is a very clever man. He knows how to play the law and the system. If the police have tried many times and failed to put him away, what makes you think you can?'

Ruby's voice came down the phone loud and angry. He could hear the indignation in it.

'I am not constrained by the red tape and human rights shit that the police have to deal with.'

'That may be so, Ruby, but this is the UK, not the USA. You don't just waltz in and take a man like Keating down without repercussions. After all you have been through, do you really need this?'

He heard her sigh on the other end of the line.

'It's exactly because of what I have gone through that I need to do this. I will work with the police and whatever other official channels I have to. And I will be careful. I know how to do my job. It would be ethically wrong of me just to go back home and pretend justice has been done and let people like Keating walk scot free, doing what they like and flaunting the law to peddle drugs and ruin other people's lives.

'Do nothing, and my brother died in vain. I need to feel vindicated. It's my job to expose people like this. As I've already said, I have the resources available to me. I can't just walk away from all this and draw a line under it. That's not me, Tony.'

He realised that her mind was made up. She was as stubborn as a mule. Again, like father, like daughter, some might say.

'Ruby, I know men like Keating. Believe me, he won't go down without a fight.'

'That's why I need you and your expertise in my corner. You are still in my corner, Tony?'

He gritted his teeth and took a deep breath as he felt emotion welling up inside of him.

'For Christ's sake, you are my daughter. Of course, I'm in your corner. I want to get to know you better and have a proper relationship with you, but I don't want to risk losing you now that I know you exist. I have nothing left of worth in my life but you. I ask you not to do anything rash and keep me in the loop. Promise me.'

When she spoke, her voice had softened.

'I would like to get to know you better, too. So, I give you my word, I will be careful. I am going to speak to Richmond and then to my colleagues back home on the paper about my plans, and start digging into Keating's businesses. I'll also look at past legal cases against him that didn't stick in court.'

'How can I help?' asked Tony.

'You can help by looking into his background and get the word on the street about him and his firm. Can you do that?'

'I am waiting for a phone call from a colleague who thinks he knows somebody down here in Bristol who can dish the dirt on Keating. I'll see what I can come up with. I'll be in touch.'

'Okay, Tony. And by the way,' she paused briefly, 'you take care, too.'

As the phone went dead, Tony allowed a small smile to cross his face. She cared for him. It was more than he could have hoped for.

He could not disguise the fact that he was concerned for her, but as she'd said, she was a big girl who lived and had grown up in New York. She was one tough lady, and had survived up until now without the protective arm of Tony Slade around her, so he had to cut her a little slack.

Chapter thirteen

Tony sat in Costa with a black americano coffee in front of him. He was trying to process the conversation he had just had with Ruby.

Tony understood more than most that trying to bring down a man like Keating spelt only one thing: Danger.

Some years back, Tony had reluctantly started working for the North East villain Kenny Robbins, so he had plenty of inside knowledge on how a criminal empire operated. He also had first-hand knowledge of how it could come down on you if you messed with it.

The ripples he had caused had only recently stopped spreading. Getting involved in that world again was something Tony had never wanted to consider. Not after all the pain and death it had caused. It had almost claimed his own life. He had been lucky, but still bore the bullet scars to prove it.

Just then his phone rang. Caller ID told him It was Brian James.

'Hello, Brian. Good to hear from you. What have you got for me?'

'I found a contact for you. We did some security work in Afghanistan a few years back. First-rate guy. He lives just outside Bristol. His name is Eddie Montgomery. Ex SAS. Solid and reliable. He has his ear to the ground in most areas through the security company he runs.'

Brian gave Tony a mobile number and the address of Fox Security Solutions.

'They are a top -notch outfit and work all over the world. They specialise in undercover work and hostage retention. They don't guard the door of Tesco, you know what I mean?'

'Thanks, Brian. I owe you one, mate,' said Tony.

Brian explained that he had told Eddie a bit about Tony's background and that his real identity was Tony Slade, not Tony Swan. There was no point trying to bullshit a man like Eddie. Plus, he would probably have done a background check on him anyway. Tony told him he was fine with that.

Brian reminded him that, whatever he was up to in the UK, there was always a place for him in Morocco when it was over, if he needed it. Tony thanked him once again for all his help and hung up the call.

He studied the address of the security company. It was situated in a place called Nailsea, which was around ten miles from Bristol city centre. He set the sat nav and headed for the Long Ashton bypass. Traffic permitting, it would take no more than thirty minutes. He rang the number and it was picked up almost instantly.

'Eddie Montgomery,' answered a deep Scottish accent.

'Tony Slade. Can we meet?'

Five minutes later, Tony was heading for Nailsea.

DI Richmond got the call he wanted late afternoon. The registration number was recognisable. It had been run through the motor vehicle computer and... bingo. It was registered to LK Business Associates, one of Keating's companies.

Just as he thought things could not get any better, the desk sergeant, Bob Rose, rang him.

'I got a guy out here in reception that I think you should talk to, Steve.'

Intrigued, Richmond walked out into reception and Bob Rose nodded in the direction of a man sat on a bench in the corner.

'Albert Sweet, Steve. According to him, he was on the station the night Gary Carter died. He says he filmed the footage of the altercation on his phone.

'Okay, Albert. Can I call you, Albert?'

Richmond did not wait for a reply but ploughed right on.

'Tell me exactly what you told the desk sergeant.'

They were sat across a table from each other in interview room number one.

Albert Sweet was sixty-nine years of age. He was pretty unremarkable really. Grey hair, grey suit, grey personality. He worked for the local council in the planning department.

Sweet pulled out an old iPhone4 inside a battered red leather case. Richmond did not think anybody still had an iPhone as early as this. He just hoped it worked properly.

He showed Richmond the footage of the fight Carter had had with the three boys. Well, it was not really a fight, more like one-way traffic for Carter. What really interested Richmond was what was said after the incident, when the three boys had picked themselves up off the floor.

They postured and threatened Carter with the names Ice Squad and Lenny Keating. The words could be heard as clear as a bell. Fucking jackpot.

This footage and the Land Rover's registration might just be enough to bring charges.

'Can I ask, Albert, why you took so long to come forward with this?'

'I have been on holiday in Spain and forgot about it. It was not until I came home and was downloading my holiday photos that I found it again. I didn't realise how vital it was until I read about the man being pushed to his death.'

'Didn't you see that as well?' asked Richmond.

'No. You see, I left the station platform after the fight. I was a bit frightened, to be honest, as I got quite close to film the scene and I thought one of those thugs might see me and take the phone away. Anyway, I was only there to train spot, not to catch a train."

Richmond's eyes widened.

'What? At that time of night? Are you kidding me?'

Albert Sweet's face reddened, and he coughed.

'No, it's the truth. It's a passion of mind. My father used to work on the old steam engines as a driver, and sometimes he would let me ride with him, and that's how I fell in love with the railway. I only live a few minutes away and go over to the station at numerous times of the day. You see, different engines come and go all the time and I was particularly interested in seeing engine number—'

Richmond cut him off.

'Okay, thank you, Albert. We'll need to keep your phone for a day or so to download the recording. Are you okay with that?'

'Of course, Detective Inspector. I find this all remarkably interesting.'

Richmond got up from his seat.

'Right. Very well, Albert. Come back out to reception and we will just get you to fill a form in to authorise us having your phone. It shouldn't take too long. I'll organise a cup of coffee for you.'

Albert Sweet got up.

'Tea for me, please. Milk. No sugar. I don't drink coffee. Irritates my lower bowel.'

Inwardly, Richmond thought to himself, *What a wet fucking fart*. But he had to admit, he could have kissed the bloke when he'd seen what he had captured on his phone.

The railway CCTV footage had been inconclusive, plus it had no audio.

This video on Sweet's phone was like gold dust. The dialogue was as clear as a bell.

After leaving Albert, Richmond saw Sergeant Luke Drury coming in through the main door.

'Luke, my son, have I got some good news to tell you! You will not fucking believe it. Come into my office.'

Tony and Eddie hit it off straight away. Most ex-forces do. There was always a special bond.

Eddie Montgomery was in his early sixties, and stood around 6ft tall. He was lean and suntanned, with tightly cropped steel grey hair that matched the colour of his eyes. The suntan was due to a recent visit to Iraq. Eddie did not elaborate on this, and Tony did not ask.

Over a coffee in Eddie's office, Tony filled him in on his background. Eddie, in turn, explained how he had set up his successful security company, and Tony was not surprised that his old friend Doug Jacobs had given Eddie an initial loan to help him out.

That was what the late Doug Jacobs had done for any mates coming out of the services with no job or prospects. Some of the guys had crashed and burned, but Eddie was a shining example of one of the successful ones.

He had twenty-five men working directly for him, and a solid network across the country. They worked all over the world.

Eddie had a strong background in the army, finishing with the 22nd SAS regiment. He was one of the 35-strong SAS team of Operation Nimrod that took out the terrorists in the 1980 Iranian Embassy in London. He was British royalty in Tony's eyes. He could have talked all day to the man, but they needed to get down to business.

Tony asked about Lenny Keating. Eddie told him that Keating owned two nightclubs in Bristol – *Roxy's and Snow White's*. They were legit firms but fronted a drugs racket. He went on to say that Keating was very smart and had so far managed to avoid any prosecution. Word was that he had certain policemen and lawyers in his back pocket.

He lived in a penthouse flat overlooking the docks, but could usually be found at one of his clubs or at the *Raw Power* gym. He was fanatical about training.

Tony noted this.

Eddie took a sip of coffee and then continued, 'He has a lot of people working for him. Young girls and boys doing drugs runs. Criminal gangs across the UK seem to be trafficking more children, some as young as eleven, to transport their wares. They are being targeted via social media, across schools, foster homes, and homeless shelters, with the promise of money or notoriety. At the end of the day, they are just expendable.'

Tony had listened intently to what Eddie had just said, and thought back to his earlier conversation with Ruby. That was what she had been trying to get across to him, that the three boys' deaths did not stop the root cause of the problem. It was evil men like Keating who were the real problem and they had to be stopped. The police had their hands tied with red tape and human rights bollocks. They were stifled.

'Who has Keating got close to him, Eddie?'

'He has an inner firm of trusted lieutenants. They are "Mad" Micky Stone, Big Will Joseph, and his top boy, Joel Sterling. One or more of them is always by his side. They are tight. They are also stone-cold killers. Not many people want to fuck with them.'

'Have you got photos of them?' asked Tony.

Eddie smiled.

'Yeah, I'll print those off for you now. Got plenty of shots of them from CCTV around the city. Keating mainly deals in weed but will also dabble in coke and pills. Him and his crew will definitely be "carrying at all times". There is a guy he deals with for his hardware when needed. His name is Ronnie Patterson – a bodybuilder at the same gym as Keating, *Raw Power*. He is also a doorman at the *Jungle Hut* club and deals on the doors. He is a small cog in the workings, but a useful one when it comes to firearms.'

Tony saw Eddie hesitate a moment.

'What is it, Eddie? What else?'

'Tony, I know your background. I know all about you getting shot in that coffee shop.'

'So? What about it? What do you know?'

'Remember that lunatic Colin Crane who shot up the coffee house?' asked Eddie.

Tony's heart skipped a beat. *Remember it? How could he forget it?* He was there when it happened and one of only a few to survive it. He tried to keep a rein on his emotions.

'Yeah, I do happen to recall it.'

'Well,' continued Eddie, 'word in the know is this Ronnie Patterson provided the Uzi for the nutcase.'

Tony digested the information. He felt a pulsing in his temples and adrenaline began to course through his body. This Patterson guy was the man who had supplied Colin Crane with a firearm. The firearm that caused murder and mayhem in the coffee house and ultimately led to the death of his sweet precious Annette, and almost his own.

He had tried so hard to push the terrible events he had witnessed to the back of his mind, and now he was being told who had supplied the firearm that had been responsible for so many pointless and tragic deaths, including that of the woman he'd loved.

Tony felt something shift in him. The dark side that he had managed to bury for some while was now returning. His mind shifted gears. He knew what needed to be done.

'Tony, are you okay?'

Eddie's voice brought him back from his reverie. Tony looked at the concerned features of the other man.

'Jesus, you look like you have just seen a ghost. You sure you're alright?'

Tony's face broke into a forced smile.

'Yes, I'm fine, Eddie. How accurate is this information?'

Eddie looked at Tony intently.

'As good as it gets. Look, my friend. I know it's none of my business, but if you are planning on going up against this Keating geezer or paying a visit to Patterson, that is your business. I don't want to know. I can't afford to be connected in any way to it. You understand?'

Tony nodded. 'I understand that, Eddie. I'm more than thankful for the information you've provided.'

Eddie smiled.

'Okay, that's settled. Now, you are going to need some hardware of your own. Am I right?'

'Yes, you're right, Eddie.'

He got up from his chair.

'Here are the photos. I've written the names of the face on each image.'

Tony took the photos and briefly studied them. As Eddie had said a moment ago, these guys were hard core criminals.

'Right. Follow me,' said Eddie.

The two men headed out of the office and the building in which it was housed then walked across a large gravelled expanse of car park to another large warehouse. Inside, there was a variety of expensive cars, a few Range Rovers, and half a dozen vans of different shapes and sizes.

'Work vehicles, depending on the needs of the client, from chauffeuring to surveillance to battle bus,' explained Eddie.

They moved to a steel door at the back of the building that had a keypad on the wall next to it.

'Sorry, Tony. Do you mind looking the other way for a second?' asked Eddie.

Tony obliged. It was like something out of a James Bond movie.

Eddie keyed in a code and the door slid smoothly open. He flipped on a wall switch and the inside was bathed in pure white light.

'Welcome to my armoury,' Eddie gestured with his hand.

Tony let his eyes appraise the room. It was exactly like something from a James Bond movie.

'Fucking hell, Eddie. Are you planning World War Three?'

The other man chuckled. 'Got to be prepared for every emergency, my friend.'

The room contained an array of weaponry from handguns, rifles, and shotguns, to machine guns, grenades, and even portable rocket launchers. It was a right Aladdin's cave for the budding Rambo.

'We have some pretty heavy-duty contracts all over the world, Tony. Needs must, so they say.'

Tony nodded. He understood.

'Right then, what are you looking for?' asked Eddie.

Tony walked across to a table of handguns.

'I need something portable, not too awkward to carry, and has stopping power.'

Eddie smiled.

'Sounds like you are describing my ex-missus. Okay, what about this?'

He held up a Glock 17.

'Reliable, lightweight, and packs a punch. 9mm, seventeen rounds in clip. You familiar with it?'

Tony nodded. 'Yeah, we have met before.'

'Good. Then I would definitely recommend it. Now, as a back-up, I suggest this baby.'

He reached for another gun from the table.

'This is a CZ 75B 9mm semi-automatic made in the Czech Republic. Once again, lightweight, easy to carry, quicker to pull out. A good reliable shooter. Weighs 2.2 pounds. Holds a clip of sixteen.'

Tony handled the gun. It did feel light and comfortable.

'Okay, I'm sold. I'll take them both.'

'Good choices,' said Eddie.

He opened a large drawer that contained an impressive array of knives, then reached in and pulled one out.

'This is the Cold Steel 39LSFC leatherneck. Made of German D2 steel, with a non-reflective black powder coating. 6¾ inch blade. Overall knife size, 11¾ inches. An absolute beauty.'

He passed it to Tony, who took the knife and weighed it up in his hand. It was a precision-made killing tool. No doubt about it.

'Always nice to have a blade to fall back on, so to speak,' said Eddie.

'Right, Eddie. I'll take these three items and half a dozen boxes of ammo. What's the damage?'

'We will talk money later, my friend. No rush. My only request is that, when they have done their job, you dispose of them carefully. Do not be tempted to hang on to any. Understand?'

'Perfectly,' replied Tony.

'Most of the guns you see in here are legal, and licensed for the business. The ones I have shown you are not. They originate from Central and Eastern Europe, consolidated in Belgium or the Netherlands before transiting into the UK via France. I suspect our friend Ronnie Patterson does it the same way. They are virtually impossible to trace, but they need to be disposed of correctly. My suggestion is water. Many a river or sea contains many secrets.'

'Understood, Eddie. Thank you for all your help,' said Tony.

Eddie shook Tony's hand.

'No problem. If you need anything else or want to know something, call me.'

Five minutes later, Tony was in his car and heading back to Bristol, with the weapons safely stashed in the tyre well of the boot.

He felt a lot better to have them. He hoped they were only there as a last resort, but if he had to go into Keating's territory, he needed to be prepared.

Tony's military training and experience in some of the world's hot zones made him well aware of what he needed to do if things turned ugly.

Chapter fourteen

DI Richmond knocked on the door of Chief Superintendent Timothy Hardwick's office. He could not wait to tell the bastard about the latest developments on the case.

And not only about the evidence discovered. An hour or so previously, as he had been filling Luke Drury in on his findings, Ruby Carter had rung to say that she wanted to use her influence in the press to work with him to nail Keating and shut down his operation.

He was all for that, and had given her the number of Susie Rawlings at *The Daily News*. He told her he thought they would make a great team. They could all liaise to bring the bastard to rights.

Things were looking good for Richmond. He deserved this break. He needed it.

'Come in,' came a voice from beyond the door.

The office was what you might expect of a man of Hardwick's rank. It was clean and bright, all polished wood and brass. Hardwick sat behind a large desk that had a sparse scattering of things on top of it, but each item had obviously been carefully placed.

Hardwick carried on signing off the forms which he was working on, without acknowledging the fact that the DI had entered the room. Richmond coughed uncomfortably. Finally, Hardwick looked up as he put the cap on his fancy rolled gold pen.

'Ah, Steve. Right, what can I do for you?'

'I thought you might like an update on the Gary Carter case. We have had a few significant break-throughs.'

Hardwick gestured to a leather chair in front of his desk.

'Please take a seat. What have we got then? Good news, I hope?'

Steve Richmond sat down with a small smile playing on his lips.

'Well, we have confirmed that the Range Rover spotted at the site of the murders of Lewis and Riggs, belonged to Keating, and we now have mobile phone footage from a gentleman called Albert Sweet at the railway station, which shows Harvey Banks clearly stating he worked for Keating. We can now confirm from that recording, and the station's CCTV footage, that it was definitely Banks who pushed Gary Carter to his death.'

Hardwick sat back in his chair with a look of surprise on his face.

'Well, this certainly is good news.'

'There's more yet, sir,' said Richmond.

Lenny Keating answered his mobile. He was in his office at *Roxy's*.

'About time you rang. What have you got for me?'

'You need to report your Range Rover missing. The police have your registration number at the scene of the two kids' murders. Take it somewhere and burn it out fast.'

Keating listened intently.

'Okay, that will be done right away. What else?'

'Phone footage from a witness at the train station the night of Carter's death shows Harvey Banks shouting to anybody who was listening that he worked for you.'

'This phone evidence, where is it now?'

'It's safe. I've pulled it.'

Keating chuckled down the phone line.

'Good fucking work, my man. You wouldn't happen to have details of where this witness lives, would you?'

'Yes, I do, Lenny. But keep things fucking discreet, okay?'

'Chill, my man. I will personally sort it.'

'Oh, and there is one more thing. Ruby Carter, the sister of Gary, is not about to return to America, even though she knows that the boys who were responsible for pushing her brother have died. She is going to use her clout with her newspaper to bring you down. She ultimately holds you responsible for what happened. I've looked into her background. She has some pull, and she will come for you hard.'

Keating digested the news. The fucking bitch was opening a whole can of worms. He could not afford the attention. He had some big plans in the pipeline. Plans that would go pear-shaped if this Ruby Carter and the police came after him.

'Where is this woman staying at present?' asked Keating.

'Now hang on, Lenny. This is Bristol, for fuck's sake, not the Wild West. I can't tell you that. I am risking too much as it is.'

Keating's voice changed and the menace in it was as clear as day.

'Now you listen to me, son. I fucking own you. You are in this way too deep to start giving me ultimatums. You will tell me where she is, and you will get a good bonus. That should keep that little princess of a wife of yours happy for another while. The cash will stop her burning your fucking credit cards. It will keep her and your lovely daughter in the luxury they are used to. So, don't fuck me about. Let's have Ruby Carter's whereabouts right now.'

Sergeant Luke Drury hung up the call after giving Lenny Keating the name of the hotel where Ruby Carter was staying. He did not feel good about himself for doing it, but he had no choice. As Keating had correctly pointed out, he was in too deep.

He had been on Keating's payroll for a year now. He had money problems. Well, he didn't personally, but his wife Tessa certainly did. In fact, she thought it grew on fucking trees.

Tessa Drury, née Bryant, was an ex-underwear model and occasional Page Three girl. His mates told him that he was punching above his weight when he married her, and they were right. And the kudos that came from being married to an incredibly beautiful woman had made it all worth it, even her outlandish spending.

She had been used to the good life, earning a lot of money from her modelling, but she had made some bad money investments and had lost the lot. Luke knew about this when they first met, but had stupidly thought that he could look after her needs. He was still paying off money for their wedding and their honeymoon in Bali. Tessa had really gone to town on that one. Then came the clothes shopping obsession and endless beauty treatments.

Once she got pregnant and little Alice was born, she had to cultivate the image of the perfect 'yummy mummy'. Only the best for her and Alice.

As the debts had mounted up, Drury had been sinking. Then, out of the blue, came an opportunity to wipe those debts.

One night around 11:30pm, quite by chance he had been driving, off duty, past a deserted industrial site when he came across two cars parked up in the shadows of one of the units. Something about them did not sit right with him, so he'd pulled over and quietly walked towards the vehicles.

As he got closer, he saw one of the cars, a Mercedes, had the boot open and two men were busy rooting around in it. They did not notice Drury until he was right on them producing his warrant card and announcing that he was from the police. The two men were caught cold and bang to rights. In the boot was a stash of cocaine and a briefcase with £50,000 in it.

Drury recognised one of the men as being Lenny Keating. The man had been as cool as a cucumber and had suggested to Drury that they could strike a deal. He proposed that Drury let the other man walk with the coke, and let Keating drive away, then Drury could take the briefcase and its contents. Job done. Nobody would ever know.

At that time, Drury was at his most vulnerable. His credit cards were maxed out and he had no available ready cash. This was the answer to his prayers, so he took the bribe and left with the briefcase.

It was just as well he did, because unknown to him, all the time Keating had been talking to him, he'd had a gun in his coat pocket trained on Drury just in case he did not go for the deal.

The joy was only short-lived, though, as Tessa did not curb her spending habits. Drury knew he should have been stronger and stood up to her, but he was frightened that if he did, he would lose both her and Alice.

So, he'd found Keating down at the *Raw Power* gym and basically sold him his soul for money. He hated himself for doing it, but he was trapped. From then on, he began to feed Keating useful titbits to keep the heat off him, in exchange for money.

None of his work colleagues suspected anything. Drury had a sharp Oxford-educated brain to stay one step ahead of the game. Working with DI Richmond, and becoming his friend, ensured that he was on the cutting edge of any vital news.

So, when Richmond had called him into his office earlier and told him about linking the Range Rover to Keating and the phone evidence from Albert Sweet, he had been in the right place at the right time.

When Richmond told Drury to take Sweet's phone over to the tech guys and get the video downloaded, he could not believe his luck.

When he got to the lab, the only person in there was Harriet Grey, and she was engrossed in studying what looked like a pile of old clothes laid out on one of the examining benches. She barely looked up, only to see him holding up the phone.

'Is that the phone that Steve wants me to look at?'

'Yes, it is, Harriet. I can see you're busy. I'll leave it over on your desk. That okay?'

Harriet's head was down, examining something or another of interest.

'That would be great, Luke. Thank you. Sorry, I can't stop. This is important. I'll check it out in a little while.'

'No worries.'

Drury walked over to her desk and stood there for a moment. He then checked that Harriet was still busy. She was, so he pocketed the phone and left, calling out a quick goodbye.

After leaving the lab, he went out into the car park and made the phone call to Keating. He did not want to give up Ruby's whereabouts, but when all was said and done, he had to save his own ass. How could he have predicted that she would go on a one-woman crusade?

As soon as he was put on this case and the Ice Squad gang had been mentioned, he had known that it would all lead to Keating. So, along with seemingly trying to get to the bottom of the crime, he had also been stalling it in small ways to keep the heat from Keating. However, these latest developments meant that things were getting out of hand. He feared that if Keating was pulled in for murder, he would look for a plea bargain by offering Drury up and hanging him out to dry.

An hour after Drury and Keating's phone conversation, Joel Sterling walked into Bridewell Police Station, went up to front desk, and informed Bob Rose that he wanted to report the theft of a black Range Rover.

He told the desk sergeant that he had only just discovered it missing from outside his house as he had been away for a few days. Sergeant Luke Drury heard the conversation and told Bob Rose that he would take it from there and ushered Sterling into an interview room.

'Right, Joel. Fill this form in and make sure your story is airtight, and then get the fuck out of here. Have you disposed of the vehicle?'

Joel Sterling's face split into a beaming grin.

'As we speak, brother, as we speak. No sweat.'

When the paperwork was done, Drury ushered Sterling towards the door.

'Oh, by the way, Luke, the boss wants you to send a photo of this Ruby Carter over to his phone asap. We want to make sure that, when we pay her a little visit, we get the right girl.'

Drury gritted his teeth. It took all his self-control not to punch Sterling in his stupid grinning mouth. He pushed the man out of the door.

'He'll get it. Now get out of here.'

When Sterling had left the station, Drury went into the washroom, entered an empty toilet cubicle, and sent the photo to Keating. He then headed to DI Richmond's office and knocked on the open door.

'Got a minute, Gov?'

Richmond looked up from his work.

'Yes, sure. What is it, Luke?'

'You aren't going to believe this, but one of Keating's employees has just waltzed in here and reported the Range Rover stolen. Said he had been out of town for a few days, just got back and noticed it was gone.'

Richmond's face said it all.

'You are fucking kidding me?'

Drury shook his head. Richmond stood up.

'The cheeky fucker. Is he still here?'

'No, Gov. I took the statement and he's gone.'

'Gone? Why the fuck didn't you hold him?'

'On what charge?'

Richmond was flustered.

'I don't know. Anything. Being a lying fucker for one.'

'Look, Gov, I didn't think I should arouse his suspicions to what we have on Keating in case he went back there and told him, and they all did a disappearing act.'

Richmond nodded and sat back down. He seemed a little calmer.

'Alright. Yeah, that makes sense.'

Drury relaxed a little. Then Richmond looked up.

'How the fuck did he know we were onto him? We didn't release any news about the Range Rover seen at the murder site or any eyewitnesses. How the fuck did he know?'

'Maybe he's telling the truth,' replied Drury.

The look Richmond gave him made him hurriedly add, 'Only joking, Gov.'

'Very funny, Luke. You drop the phone down to Harriet?'

'Yes. She was busy when I got there. I left it. She said she would look at it when she finished what she was doing.'

'Right. I'll give her a call in a little while. If that fucker Keating maintains his vehicle was stolen, then as it stands, the only hard evidence that will hold up in court will be the video and Sweet's testimony. Luke, just out of curiosity, drive around to Sweet's house and check that everything is okay.'

"You think he is in danger?"

'Maybe. I'm not sure, but I don't want to take any chances."

'Okay, Gov. I'm on my way.'

'Ring me as soon as you check him out.'

Drury nodded.

Albert Sweet heard his doorbell ring. He moved his cat from his lap and got up out of his armchair. He grabbed the remote and aimed it at the television, turning down the volume on 'Countdown'.

He walked into the hallway of his small ground-floor flat and saw a silhouette through the glass panel of his front door. The bell sounded again.

'Okay, I'm coming,' called Albert. 'Who is it?'

'Parcel for you, sir. Needs signing.'

Parcel, thought Albert, *I can't remember ordering anything*. Unless maybe his daughter Carol had remembered his birthday this year, and sent a gift all the way from Australia. *Better late than never*, he supposed.

Albert opened the door unexpectedly to 'Mad' Micky Stone.

'Are you Mr Albert Sweet?'

Albert replied yes, but could not see any parcel. And this man did not seem to be dressed like a delivery man. He was confused. Then he saw the knife in the man's hand.

Albert tried to shut the door, but 'Mad' Micky barged his way in, pushing Albert to the ground. Micky slammed the front door shut and loomed over Albert as the older man sank to the floor in terror.

'Okay, grandad. Let's try and get this over with as quickly as possible, shall we? Don't try and fight me. You won't win.'

Micky straddled the older man and started the job by driving the wicked looking blade into Albert Sweet's chest while his other hand clammed down on his mouth to stifle the scream.

DI Richmond's desk phone rang, and he picked it up. It was Harriet Grey on the other end.

'Steve, I'm about to look at the phone that was left here, but I can't find it anywhere. Did you or Luke pick it up again for some reason?'

'No, Luke brought it down when he spoke to you and left it per my instructions. Are you sure it's not been moved or under something? At the moment, that phone is more important than the holy grail."

'No, I've searched my whole desk and it isn't there.'

Richmond knew Harriet was excellent at her job and unlikely to have made a mistake. Something did not feel right.

'Shit. Okay, leave it with me, Harriet, and I'll check with Luke when I see him.'

Richmond hung up. He sat deep in thought. First, the news that the Range Rover was apparently stolen. Now, the phone with crucial evidence goes missing. What the fuck was going on?

He rang Luke Drury's phone, but it went to voicemail. He left a message telling him to ring him as soon as he picked up the call.

Lenny Keating and Big Will Joseph walked into the foyer of the Ravenscroft Hotel. They were both dressed smartly in suit, shirt, and tie. They moved to the reception.

A young woman was the only person on duty at that moment. Keating flashed a fake police warrant card.

'DI Richmond and Sergeant Luke Drury here to see Ms Ruby Carter.'

Drury had supplied him with the name of the lead policeman on the case who was also responsible for looking after Ruby Carter.

'Right. Okay. I'll give her room a ring and check that she is in. May I ask what you want to see her for?'

'Official police business. Can you just make the call...' Keating squinted at the girl's name badge, 'please, Kelly?'

She hurriedly rang the number. The two men seemed to have an air of menace about them.

'Hello. This is Kelly on reception, Ms Carter. There are two policemen here to see you. A DI...?'

She looked towards the two men, who repeated their names to her. Kelly then relayed them down the phone.

She finally put the phone down. 'Okay, gentlemen. She said to go right on up to her room. It is number 101 on the third floor. The lifts are over to your left.'

'Thank you very much for your time, Kelly,' said Keating.

As the men moved towards the lifts, the girl breathed a sigh of relief. There was something about them that made her feel uncomfortable, and she was glad to see them move off.

The lift started climbing. Both men silently watched the floor numbers rising. Then Keating spoke.

'Funny coincidence she is in room 101?'

Will regarded him.

'How do you mean, boss?'

'You know. Room 101, *1984*, George Orwell.'

Will looked blankly back at Keating, as if he were speaking Arabic.

'George who?'

Keating shook his head.

'Never mind, Will. Forget it.'

The big man went to speak, but the lift suddenly pinged and came to a stop. They both got out and looked at the numbers on the wall.

'To the left,' pointed Keating.

Outside room 101, they checked the corridor both ways. It was clear. They now drew their guns and held them low, discreetly covered in both hands.

'Now, remember, we are going to snatch her and see if we can talk a little sense into her. If not, then she is going to make a hell of a hostage and maybe an alternative route to get ourselves out of this mess, so don't fucking shoot her.'

Big Will looked wounded.

'I know, boss. I know what you said.'

Keating knocked on the door, which was almost immediately opened by Ruby Carter.

'I wasn't expecting you, Detective...'

Her words froze in her throat as she realised that this was not who she had been expecting. The two big men pushed their way into the room and shut and locked the door. Keating aimed his gun at Ruby.

'Allow me to introduce myself. My name is Lenny Keating. I believe you would like to talk to me.'

Ruby's surprise turned to fear. She pushed over a chair, ran to the bathroom, and slammed the door shut, turning the lock. She fished her phone out of her pocket and hit Tony Slade's number.

As she waited for him to answer, the door shook on its hinges as one of the men kicked it. It splintered but held.

She then heard Tony's voice as he answered her call.

Another huge bang sounded, and the door smashed from the hinges in an explosion of compressed cardboard and wood. Ruby flinched away and screamed, but at the same time, she had the presence of mind to throw her phone into the shower cubicle. It was still connected.

Keating loomed over her.

'Now that's not very friendly. Good old Lenny Keating thought he would save you the bother of finding him and come to you, and this is the thanks he gets.'

Keating nodded at Big Will. He reached out and grabbed Ruby by the hair before sticking a gun in her face. She cried out in pain.

Keating ignored her and continued, 'You and I are going to have a nice long chat, but not here. You are coming with us without any fucking fuss, or Will here will hurt you badly. Do you understand me?'

'Yes,' replied Ruby.

'Right, follow me and don't try anything cute.'

The two men and Ruby left the room.

The phone lay undetected in the shower cubicle. Tony Slade was listening on the other end and knew exactly what was happening.

DI Richmond picked up his mobile and rang Drury's number again. No answer. Where the fuck was he? Surely, he had checked on Sweet by now.

He decided to give Ruby Carter's number a call as well, but it just had an engaged tone. He wanted to arrange to meet her and give her the latest update on the case. He tried her number again, but with no success.

Frustrated, he thought he would ring the hotel directly and see if she was in. Maybe she was ringing home or something? He dialled the reception of the Ravenscroft.

'Hello, Ravenscroft Hotel. Kelly speaking. How may I help?'

'Yes. Hello. I wonder if it might be possible to speak to Ms Carter?'

'Oh, sorry, I think she has company at present. May I ask who is calling, please?'

'Yes, of course. My name is DI Richmond.'

There was silence on the end of the phone.

'Hello. Hello, are you there?' asked Richmond.

Kelly spoke again.

'Yes. I'm sorry, but there seems to be a bit of confusion.'

'How do you mean?'

'Well, at present, there is a DI Richmond and a Sergeant Drury on their way up to see Ms Carter.'

Richmond's heart skipped a beat.

'Kelly, listen carefully. What did these men look like?'

'Well, to be honest, they were quite intimidating. They were both smartly dressed black men. Big, like bodybuilders, and—'

Richmond cut her off.

'Ring the room number now, please.'

'I don't understand,' stuttered Kelly.

Richmond shouted down the phone.

'Just ring the room number NOW.'

Richmond waited. He was suddenly sweating. Kelly came back on the line.

'It is ringing and ringing, but no answer. But I know she is definitely up there.'

Richmond cursed under his breath.

'Kelly, have you a chief of security there?'

'Yes, we have.'

'Put him on the phone right now.'

A couple of seconds later, the chief of hotel security, Mike Gregory, came on the line. Richmond filled him in on the situation and told him to watch the exits. He warned him that both men were probably armed. If he could contain them in the hotel, Richmond was on his way.

'Can you do that, Mike?'

'Yes, Detective Inspector. My team and I will get on to it. We—'

The phone suddenly went dead.

'Mike? Mike? Can you hear me?'

Richmond was answered by silence. *Shit, he was too late.*

'Drop the phone and don't fucking move, or I will blow your brains out. Do you understand?'

Mike Gregory nodded.

Lenny Keating pushed the gun to his head and ushered him into the back office where Kelly was already cowering on the floor in the corner.

'I want you to wipe the security tapes right now for the last hour.'

Gregory thought about refusing, but he stared at the ominous black barrel of the gun pointed at him and he did as he was told.

'Now, switch off the CCTV and unplug the system.'

Again, Gregory hesitated. Keating sensed it.

'Don't fuck with me, man. Just do it.'

Gregory complied.

'Give me your mobile phone.'

The man handed it over.

Keating pushed him into the corner.

'Sit down and don't fucking move.'

Gregory sank to the floor.

Keating dropped the phone on the carpet and crushed it into a mess with his boot. Kelly's was already next to it in the same state.

Keating moved to the computer that operated the CCTV, and in a show of brute strength, ripped the plug off the wiring so that it could not be connected up again in a hurry. He then ripped out the phone wiring as well.

'Right, I am locking you in here. No fucking heroics. We will be out of here in a few minutes and everything will be cool.'

Keating pulled the door closed and turned the key. He turned to face Big Will, who had Ruby grabbed tightly with a gun jammed into the small of her back. A small group of hotel guests was huddled into the bar. Keating addressed them.

'Stay where you are, and nobody will get hurt.'

He gestured towards the door. Big Will, holding Ruby tight, followed him outside. Minutes later, they were back in their vehicle and speeding away from the hotel.

Richmond flung his jacket on and ran out of his office. He spied Luke Drury coming through the door.

'Where the fuck have you been, and why didn't you answer your phone?'

Drury went to speak, but Richmond cut him off.

'Never mind. Later. Listen up. Keating is fucking snatching Ruby from the hotel. We have to take it they are armed. As far as I can ascertain, there are two of them. Call the firearms unit now and get them down there. Also, sign us both out handguns and get to the hotel asap!'

Before Drury could answer, his boss was running for the front door.

Chapter fifteen

Tony Slade had heard the whole conversation on the open line of Ruby's phone. As soon as the voices faded, he closed his mobile shut and headed to the wardrobe in his hotel room.

The adrenaline was beginning to course through his veins and he embraced it like an old friend. The switch had been flipped. He was now slipping into combat mode. A job had to be done. That scum Keating had his daughter, and he trusted nobody but himself to get her back.

He took off his tracksuit and pulled on a black t-shirt and black jeans. He slipped the scabbard of the leather-neck knife onto his belt and moved it around to the small of his back where his coat would cover it. Next, he strapped a double holster across his chest, and checked both loads in the Glock 17 and the CZ before slotting them snuggly in place.

He then slipped on a pair of Timberland boots and tied them tightly. Finally, he pulled on a dark navy-blue North Face Triclimate jacket. In the zipped pockets, he put spare ammo magazines, his phone, and an old friend of his that he had smuggled through UK customs – an extendable steel baton. He zipped up the jacket and pulled on a black beanie hat. He checked himself in the mirror and took a deep breath. He was ready.

Richmond brought his car to a skidding halt right outside the Ravenscroft Hotel with the siren blaring. The firearms unit van pulled up minutes later, followed by Luke Drury. A small team of officers climbed out, all armed with Heckler & Koch MP5 Carbines.

A big man approached Richmond.

'Are you SIO' he asked.

'Yes, DI Richmond.'

'I am the strategic firearms officer, Bill Casper. What have we got?'

Richmond quickly filled him in on the information he had received.

'Right, this is the way we'll play it,' said Casper.

Just then, the hotel door opened and out came chief of security Mike Gregory. His hands were raised. Once Keating had left the hotel, one of the security team had unlocked the office door, allowing Kelly and Gregory to get out.

'I am Mike Gregory, hotel chief of security. The two men have gone with a Ms Ruby Carter. My men have checked the premises. It is clean.'

'How long ago did they leave?' asked Richmond.

'About fifteen minutes ago.'

'Any ideas on where they might be going?'

'I'm sorry. They said nothing.'

'Did you see the vehicle they left in?' asked Richmond.

Gregory's face flushed.

'No. I'm afraid they locked us in the office. It all happened so fast,' he replied sheepishly.

'Anybody hurt?'

'No. A few people are shaken up, but otherwise okay.'

'Right, thank you. You can go back to your business for now, although we might well contact you later.'

'Oh, by the way, one of my men found Ms Carter's mobile phone in the shower. It may be of some use to you.'

'Thank you,' said Richmond, taking the phone.

Gregory nodded and went back inside.

Casper regarded Richmond.

'Any idea yourself where they've gone?'

Richmond shook his head.

'They could be fucking anywhere. I know a few of their haunts, but it will only be guesswork. Look, thanks for your help. I suggest you stand down for now, but be ready for my call if we locate Keating's whereabouts.'

Bill Casper nodded. 'Will do.' He walked back to the van to round up his team.

Luke Drury came up to Richmond's side and handed him a Glock 17 and holster. He took it from the younger man and slid it into his pocket.

'Leave your car here. I'll get somebody to pick it up and return it to the station. Come with me and let's see if we can find this bastard before he does the girl harm.'

'Gov, there is something you need to know. Sweet is dead.'

Richmond froze.

'What?'

Drury continued, 'That's where I've been and why I couldn't answer your call. He was stabbed to death in his house.'

Richmond could not believe what he was hearing. Things were going from bad to worse.

'How did anybody know about Sweet? It doesn't make sense. But I bet my pension that Keating is behind it. We have got to find this crazy bastard fast.'

He unlocked the car.

'Get in. You drive.'

He threw Drury the car keys.

Tony Slade's burner phone had no internet access, so he had pulled down the postcode of the *Raw Power* gym on the hotel computer, along with the nightclubs that Keating owned.

He reasoned that Keating snatching Ruby had not been a long planned-out scheme, but probably more spur of the moment. So, he deduced that she must be holed up at one of his haunts for the moment until he figured out what to do with her. Well, he prayed that was the case.

He used the sat nav in the hire car to get him to his first destination. As he drove, he went over the recent chain of events in his mind. As he had suspected, Keating had got to Ruby, but Tony couldn't figure out how Keating had known so quickly that Ruby was going to try to expose him. Somebody must have tipped him off. But who?

Tony was not about to lose another person close to him. Yes, he hardly knew Ruby, but she was his flesh and blood. His daughter. He was not going to let her die. Whatever had to be done to save her was going to be done.

He returned to the present as his sat nav told him that he had reached his destination. He chose to pull up in a side road across from the gym, which was housed in what had once been a church. He got out of the car and did a quick pat-down of his weapons. They were all in place.

Tony walked into the gym reception. It was empty, except for a girl behind the counter idly turning the pages of a magazine. She was dressed in tightfitting gym wear that was struggling to contain her surgically-enhanced breasts.

When she eventually looked up, Tony noticed her face had seen a bit of work, too. It was like looking at a Barbie doll. Her lapel badge told him her name was Carly.

'Hi, can I help you, love?' Carly asked.

Tony gave her his best smile.

'I wonder if you could tell me if Lenny Keating is in the gym today?'

She looked at Tony for a few seconds, sizing him up, and probably trying to suss out if he was a cop or not.

'No, love. I haven't seen him today.'

'Right,' replied Tony. 'What about Ronnie Patterson?'

'Yeah, he's in. Been here about an hour. He's squatting on the rack by the mirrors.'

Tony looked through the window to run an eye over the man.

He estimated that he was in his thirties. His head was shaved bald. He was a big guy. Impressive build. But in Tony's eyes, he was scum. He was nothing.

'Great. Do you think I could nip in and have a quick word with him?'

Carly regarded Tony suspiciously now.

'You a member?'

Tony leant over the counter.

'No, I'm not, but it is rather urgent that I speak to Ronnie. I'll only be five minutes.'

As he said this, he slipped a £20 note down on the countertop.

'I'm sure a pretty girl like yourself could turn a blind eye for a moment?'

Carly eyed the twenty.

'If my boss Dennis King comes in, he won't be pleased. I don't know...'

Tony dropped down another twenty.

'As I said, I'll only be five minutes.'

Carly looked at the other twenty and then scooped both notes up with her long manicured nails.

'Go on then, but be quick.'

Tony smiled.

'Thanks, Carly. You're a diamond.'

Tony walked towards the man at the squat rack. As he did so, he palmed the extendable baton.

Ronnie was accompanied by a young blond-haired guy who was helping spot for him.

The blond man's name was Simon – Ronnie's latest flame. He looked up as Tony approached.

Ronnie grunted and racked the Olympic bar that was bending with the weight on it. He smiled in Simon's direction.

'That's a personal best there. What do you think?'

Suddenly, Ronnie's smile faded as he became aware of Tony's presence. He postured up, flexing his pec muscles. Tony had seen it all before. It was a threat display. A subtle warning.

'Excuse me. Sorry to interrupt your training, but are you Ronnie Patterson?'

Patterson ballooned some more.

'Who's asking?'

'My name is Tony Slade. I'm looking for Lenny Keating.'

Ronnie sneered at Tony. 'I suggest you fuck off out of here, grandad, while you still can.'

Tony pushed the adrenal reaction down. He knew what was coming. After countless years on the doors, it was always the precursor to violence.

'Okay. Take it steady. No offence meant. Can I ask how much that was you squatted? It was mighty impressive.'

Patterson was momentarily caught off guard by this change of tact.

'What?' he asked.

'Weight. How many kilos was that squat?'

'Well, it was…'

Before Patterson had finished his answer, Tony flicked out the baton to full extension and backhanded it across the big man's head. Patterson staggered back clutching his skull, his face a mask of hurt and pain.

Tony took his advantage to bring the baton down across the man's right knee. Patterson howled in pain as he slumped to a seated position against the squat rack. Then Tony drove a kick into his face, bloodying his nose as it broke.

Simon moved towards him, but Tony cut him down with words as he pointed the baton at him.

'Don't fucking try it, son, or I will fucking destroy you!'

Simon stopped dead in his tracks.

'Please, whoever you are, don't hurt him any more. Please.'

Tony regarded Patterson drifting in and out of consciousness. He then returned his gaze to the young blond man.

'This man is a murdering scumbag. He supplies firearms to punters for fun. He is a class one criminal. I suggest you have nothing to do with him.'

Tony then grabbed Patterson by the windpipe.

'Keating. Where is he?'

Patterson slurred his response. He was having trouble breathing.

'Don't know, man. He isn't here. Maybe he's at one of his clubs. I don't know, honest.'

Tony searched the man's eyes for a lie but could not detect one.

'Do you remember Colin Crane?' asked Tony through gritted teeth.

He saw Patterson trying to process the name.

'Crane. He shot up the *Alpha Coffee House*. Killed a lot of people. Remember?'

There was recognition in Patterson's eyes.

'Yeah. So what?'

Tony squeezed his windpipe harder.

'I will tell you so what. He killed somebody dear to me, and he also nearly killed me. I know you supplied him with the gun that fucking did it.'

'Hey, man. I didn't know the guy was going to go off on one. He was a fucking looney tune.'

Tony spat out his next words with venom.

'So, that makes it alright, does it? You can square that away at night and sleep like a baby with all that blood on your hands?'

'Fuck you, man. I did what I did. I can't see into a crystal ball.'

Tony released his grip on Patterson's throat and stood back, looking down on the pathetic sight. All his bluff and bravado had gone like bath water down a plug hole. He drew the Glock 17 from his coat and aimed it at Patterson.

'Now you're going to know what it feels like.'

Patterson's eyes grew wide with fear and then tears began to roll down his cheeks.

'Please. Shit. I didn't know, man. Look, I'm fucking sorry. I didn't know.'

'May God have mercy on your soul, boy, but somehow I think the devil is going to take it.'

Tony squeezed the trigger of the Glock 17 and planted a bullet right between Patterson's eyes. Nearby, Simon screamed and dropped to his knees. Tony pointed the gun towards the rest of the people in the gym.

'Fucking stay back or you will get some of this as well. I am now leaving. Do not attempt to stop me.'

The small gathering of men did not move. As Tony moved towards the door, Carly appeared. She had popped outside for a crafty cigarette when she had heard the gunshot.

She took in the scene before her and saw the lifeless form of Ronnie Patterson lying against the squat rack with the top of his head missing. A young blond man sat by his side sobbing. She started screaming.

Tony moved past her, but gym owner Dennis King stood in the doorway. A large looming figure holding a baseball bat.

'What the fuck have you done? Coming into my gym and shooting it the fuck up. Who the hell do you think you are?'

Tony did not break his stride. He fired a round into King's left thigh, and the man dropped like a stone to the floor screaming in pain, clutching at his wound. Tony exited the gym without a backwards glance.

Once back in his car, he holstered the gun and pocketed the baton. He looked at his hands. They were steady. That is what army training gives you. You operate on another level.

He started the engine and tapped the postcode of *Snow White's* nightclub into the sat nav before pulling away.

Richmond let Drury drive as they headed towards the *Raw Power* gym. Drury glanced at his boss.

'Do you really think he would have brought her there?'

Richmond stared out of the windscreen. He had come to the same conclusion as Slade had done, that the kidnapping had all the hallmarks of a rushed job.

'I don't know, but it's a starting point. We know that he part-owns that place, so it is a possibility. I don't believe they have gone far. We have to try every one of his known haunts. They are the only leads we have to find the woman.'

'That's if she isn't dead already, Gov,' said Drury.

Richmond gritted his teeth.

'Let's not consider that yet. Keating is smart and must know at the moment that she is more valuable to him alive.'

Richmond reached into his pocket and pulled out Ruby's phone.

'Let's see if there's anything on here.'

He opened the calls and looked at the last one made. The timing suggested it had been done very shortly before the kidnapping. There was only a number but no name. He decided to ring it.

Tony's phone sounded. He picked it up from the passenger seat and saw the caller ID was Ruby. He answered it immediately with some hope in his heart, forgetting momentarily that she had left her phone behind.

'Ruby, is that you? Are you okay?'

Hope sank when a male voice answered.

'Who is this?'

Tony replied, 'I could ask the same question, and why have you got this phone?'

'My name is DI Richmond, Bristol CID, and if I'm not mistaken from the dulcet Geordie accent, you are Tony Slade. Well, well, well. So, you did come out of the woodwork.'

Tony Slade had a sense of *déjà vu*. He had picked up a similar mistaken mobile call from a DCI Wyatt some time ago – Richmond's boss. Tony had nothing to lose. The die had been well and truly cast. He was done running.

'Richmond, I haven't got time for any of your bullshit games. Do you know where Ruby is?'

Richmond laughed.

'Why the fuck should I tell you, Slade?'

'Because she's my daughter and one man is dead already because of the situation, and there are going to be plenty more. Now, do you know where she is?'

'No, I don't, but we're looking at Keating's well-known haunts as we speak.'

'Well, so am I, Richmond. But I am going to be looking in a different manner to you. You were meant to be looking after her and you fucked-up, so don't get in my way or fucking try to stop me.'

Richmond felt panic rising in him. He knew only too well what Slade was capable of. Another major incident on a case he was in charge of would surely mean the end of his career. Hardwick would have his balls in mint sauce.

'Slade, wait a minute...'

The phone went dead.

'Fuck. Fuck.'

He turned to Drury.

'That was Slade. He is here, and he is on a one-man killing spree to find his daughter and settle the score with Keating. We need to find him before he finds Keating; otherwise, there is going to be a bloodbath.'

Chapter sixteen

Ruby sat on a wooden chair in what looked like the cellar of a pub. In fact, she was in the beer cellar of *Roxy's* nightclub. Her hands and feet were bound. The gag she had been wearing over her mouth had been removed. Lenny Keating and Big Will stood over her.

'Well, lady. What am I going to do with you?' asked Keating, 'It was unfortunate what happened to your brother. He was an innocent party. In the wrong place at the wrong time. What can I tell you is that I could not have prevented that boy doing what he did, but I have taken care of the matter. So, I would really like you to get on a plane and go home and forget this unfortunate occurrence.'

Ruby looked him in the eye defiantly.

'You may not have personally pushed my brother to his death, but in my eyes, you are ultimately responsible. You need to answer to that, otherwise it will happen again. You exploit vulnerable kids and then just disregard them like garbage when it suits you.'

Keating smiled.

'That is one way of looking at it, or you could say I put money in the pockets of society's otherwise forgotten. Kids with no hope, no future, no education, who are living on the streets and probably going to die on the streets. Nobody gives a shit about them.'

'Well, that's where you're wrong,' she replied. 'There are people who give a shit, and by bringing people like you to the public's attention, things will change. My newspaper and others like it can be the lost voice of the children.'

Keating began to clap his hands.

'Great speech. Very commendable. I was afraid you would take this attitude. I was all for giving you a chance to walk away with your life. To go back to New York and take your anti-drugs campaign with you. Surely, there is enough to work with over there without stirring up shit here?'

Ruby felt anger well up inside.

'That may be true, but that all changed when my brother died.'

Keating was silent for a moment as if contemplating her comments.

'I am going to leave you for a while to think over what I said. Next time I come in here, I am not going to be so reasonable. Your family background has made you a valuable asset to me, and as you so plainly pointed out, I am good at exploiting people. I think a hefty ransom reward might be in order here, and if not, you will be going home to New York piece by piece. Either way, I win.'

He went to walk off when Ruby shouted at him, 'My father will be coming for me, and you better hope I am alive when he gets here.'

Keating stopped and looked back.

'Your father? Now I'm puzzled. Didn't I read your father passed away in a car accident?'

It was now Ruby's turn to smile.

'I am talking about my real father. I left my phone open and ringing on his number when you broke into my hotel room. He will have heard everything and will be coming for you.'

Keating processed the information.

'Interesting. Who is your father? The Terminator? He'll need to be.'

Big Will broke into a laugh at Keating's joke, but Ruby stared him down.

'No, he is fucking worse.'

The smile slipped from Keating's face.

'Well, in that case, I better prepare for him.'

Big Will replaced the tape over Ruby's mouth. Both men left the room, and she heard the heavy wooden door lock behind them.

Keating and Big Will started walking up the cellar steps. They were suddenly greeted at the top by a worried looking Joel Sterling.

'Boss, I just had a phone call from the gym. Some stranger just walked in there, shot Ronnie Patterson dead, and wounded Dennis. Apparently, a guy who was training with Ronnie said that this stranger was looking for you.'

Keating's eyes narrowed.

'Okay, let's get locked and loaded and ready for this joker.'

Drury pulled Richmond's car into the car park of the *Raw Power* gym, to find a police van already parked up there. PC Garrett walked forward to meet them.

'Hello, sir,' she addressed Richmond. 'You got here quickly. This has only just been reported. I just happened to be in the area with Sergeant Pritchard.'

'What the hell has happened here?' asked Richmond.

Sergeant Bob Pritchard appeared. Richmond found that quite ironic, as Pritchard had originally been in charge of the Gary Carter murder. That seemed a million years away now.

'How's the baby?' asked Richmond.

'Noisy,' replied Pritchard.

'What have we got here, Bob?'

'Well, sir. Two men shot. One dead. No apparent reason as yet. The SOCO guys are in there now.'

Richmond's blood froze. Slade had not been lying about killing somebody.

'Who's been shot, Sergeant?'

Pritchard addressed his notebook.

'Gym owner Dennis King wounded in the leg. He is stable and on his way to hospital. The dead man is small-time villain and doorman Ronnie Patterson.'

That did it for Richmond. He knew of Patterson, and he knew that he did business for Keating in one capacity or another.

'Okay, Sergeant. Ring in for another DI to get here and oversee this. I have another emergency to attend.'

Before Pritchard could question his order, Richmond was back in the car and the two detectives sped off.

'Where to now, Gov?' asked Drury.

Richmond loosened his tie.

'It's a toss-up between Keating's two nightclubs. Let's try *Snow White's*. It's the nearest.'

Drury headed the car in the direction of the nightclub, wondering how he was going to get himself out of this jam. For now, all he could do was run with it.

Tony Slade walked towards *Snow White's*. It was situated down a side street, away from the main road. The entrance door to the club opened straight out onto the road. A blue canopy hung over the door, and the light box above displayed its name. It was a nightclub/lap dancing club.

A delivery lorry was outside, and an overweight middle-aged man was wheeling in some boxes of spirits on a pair of sack trucks. Tony watched him disappear inside and then followed. He had no idea how many people were inside the building or if Keating was in residence, but he was going to find out. He unzipped the right-hand jacket pocket of his coat and gripped the extendable baton.

Tony walked into a small foyer and scanned it quickly. There was a large reception desk in front of him. To his right was a cloakroom. To his left was a closed door with a small plaque on it, reading 'Office'. Beyond the reception were double glass doors, which presumedly led into the dance floor and bar. One of the double doors was wedged open for the delivery man.

Suddenly, a guy came to the door. He was Asian. Young and fit looking. He walked out with a bounce and swagger in his stride.

'The place is shut, man. I'm going to have to ask you to leave.'

'Sorry, I was wondering if Lenny is about?' asked Tony.

The man's face took on a look of disdain.

'Who the fuck are you? You've got five seconds to answer my question or I'll throw you out.'

As the man said this, he moved closer, trying to intimidate Tony. Tony smiled sweetly and flipped out the baton to full extension and smashed it into the man's shin. He dropped to the floor like a stone.

Tony was immediately on him, administering another blow to his elbow. He knew striking the bony joints of the body was incredibly painful but not lethal. He had no real beef with this guy.

'I am going to ask you again,' he said. 'Is Keating here?'

The man looked at Tony, his face a mask of pain.

'Fuck you!' he screamed.

'Wrong answer,' replied Tony, and brought the baton down on his right ankle joint. 'Is he here?'

The man now shook his head.

'No, you crazy fuck. He isn't.'

Tony snapped the baton shut and put it back in his pocket. Just then the office door opened, and a pretty black girl exited. She was preoccupied and speaking into a mobile phone.

'All seems quiet here, Lenny. Nothing unusual...'

She then saw Hammad lying on the ground writhing in agony, and a man dressed all in black pointing a gun at her.

'Give me the phone now,' Tony said, reaching his hand out.

The girl meekly handed the phone over.

'Go back in that office and lock the door,' Tony ordered. 'Do not come out for ten minutes.'

Without a word, the girl backed away into the office.

Tony put the phone to his ear and heard a voice ask, 'Tanya, are you there? Is everything ok? Tanya, speak to me.'

'Tanya can't come to the phone right now,' Tony replied calmly, 'so I am here to tell you that I am coming for you, Keating. If you have touched one hair on Ruby's head, I will make sure you have time to die painfully and slowly.'

'Who the fuck is this? How dare you threaten me, you piece of shit? If you are coming, fucking come. I am at *Roxy's* and I am done running. Come and get me, fucker. I might just let the girl live long enough until you get here.'

As the phone went dead, Slade threw it at the wall, and it exploded into dozens of pieces. He looked down in time to see the man Hammad on the ground reaching down to his boot for a blade. Slade moved like a panther and knee-dropped the man's neck, sending him into unconsciousness.

He exited the front door just as the delivery man started to come back through with his empty sack truck. Who knew what he would make of the scene in the foyer?

As Tony Slade was pulling away from *Snow White's*, Richmond and Drury were pulling into the side road when a lorry blocked their path. Richmond reached over and blasted the car horn. There appeared to be no-one in the vehicle.

'Fucking hell,' groaned Richmond.

He got out of the car just in time to see a delivery man coming out of the club.

'Oy! You. Police. Is this your vehicle? If so, get it moving or I'll arrest you.'

The man looked up.

'Alright, mate. Take it steady. I forgot a signature for the delivery and just nipped back in to get one. I'm on my way. Anyway, if you're a copper, I suggest you get in there. The manager has just been assaulted.'

'Bollocks,' cursed Richmond under his breath.

As the lorry pulled away, Richmond signalled Drury to pull into the space outside the club. He headed to the door, already knowing he was too late.

As soon as Richmond disappeared into the club, Luke Drury produced his mobile phone and called Keating. It was answered immediately by the man himself.

'Who the fuck is this clown gunning for me?' Keating asked.

Drury spoke quickly with one eye on the club entrance.

'His name is Tony Slade. He is Ruby Carter's real blood father and he is coming for his daughter. This man is no clown. He was a highly experienced ex-paratrooper and mercenary. He is also an expert with guns, knives, and his bare hands. Do not underestimate him, Lenny.'

'Where is he now? Do you know?' replied Keating.

'Well, due to the trail of storm damage he has left at the gym and at *Snow White's*, I would hazard a guess that he is on the way to *Roxy's* right now.'

'Right. What are you doing?'

'I'm with the DI, and we will be coming your way shortly as well. Look, Lenny. Take my advice. Cut your losses, let the girl go, and get the hell out of the country while you can.'

'Listen to me, Drury. You are paid to do things for me, not give me your opinion. Me pissing off would certainly let you off the hook as well, wouldn't it? Fuck this Slade dude and fuck you and your DI. I am not about to do any running, so bring it on. Whatever happens, if I go down, you are going down with me. Now, stall your boss for as long as you can.' Keating hung up.

Drury pocketed the phone and got out of the car. The whole situation was now out of control. He could not give himself up; he would lose everything he had worked for. His job, wife, and kid. He couldn't go to prison. A copper would not last five minutes in there, especially with Keating's connections. He had to think of a way out.

He suddenly had an idea. He fished into his coat pocket and produced a four-inch folding lock knife which he always carried as a bit of back-up. So far, he had never had to use it in any altercation, but now it was perfect.

He moved to the rear driver's side wheel, and took one last glance towards the club before stabbing the blade into the tyre wall. The air hissed out angrily as it quickly deflated. He looked up and saw Richmond coming out of the club entrance, talking animatedly into his mobile and at the same time gesturing for Drury to get back in the vehicle. Richmond hung up the call and walked up to the car.

'Right, get to *Roxy's* now as fast as you can and get the siren on. I've just spoken to Bill Casper and told him to get his team over there. This is it. Our last chance to nail Keating and Slade in one go, and I am not going to fuck this one up.'

'Right, Gov, but first, I am going to have to change this flat tyre,' said Drury.

Richmond moved around the car and regarded the forlorn looking tyre.

'Bollocks!' he exclaimed. 'Please tell me we have a spare.'

'I'll check,' said Drury heading to the boot.

Just as Richmond thought this day could not get any worse, his phone rang, and he saw Chief Superintendent Hardwick's name on the screen. He would have to answer it. He had been avoiding his boss for too long.

Richmond shouted to Drury, 'Got to take this call from "Hard Dick". You'll be alright changing the tyre, won't you?'

He was already walking away before Drury could reply. As soon as Richmond was out of earshot, Drury got out his phone. He needed to make another urgent call.

Chapter seventeen

Tony Slade had parked his car in a side street a short distance away from *Roxy's,* and was making the rest of the journey on foot. Before leaving the car, he had taken a pair of M22 field binoculars out of the boot, and made his way into the public park across the road from the club.

He found a quiet place away from prying eyes and surveyed the facade of *Roxy's*. It was a large Georgian red brick structure that, in Tony's estimation, had probably been a factory of some sort back in the day. It looked like it was securely locked up and there were no cars outside.

He spotted an alleyway running up the left-hand side of the building, and there was a rusting tin sign on the wall, with an arrow pointing down the alleyway, which read 'Car Park'. He decided that would be his best option to try and find a way inside.

Furtively, he checked his weapons and then left the binoculars in the bushes. He did not need anything unnecessary weighing him down. With that in mind, he also emptied his bladder. He had learned from the old army saying of 'don't bring anything into battle you don't need'. Now he was all set.

He moved through the park and out onto the road a little way down from the club, then crossed the road.

He could now enter the alley from the side and, hopefully, nobody would see him.

A few moments later, he slipped undetected into the alley. He reached to the small of his back, unclipped the sheath, and pulled out the combat knife. It fitted snuggly into his palm.

In the cellar of *Roxy's*, Ruby was working hard to try and loosen her bonds. Her hands and feet were duct-taped, as was her mouth. And her torso was taped to the chair.

For over half an hour, she had painfully loosened the strip of tape over her mouth by repeatedly opening and closing her jaws, and working her tongue against the inside of the tape. Finally, she had managed to get her tongue under the bottom edge and worked it loose, then used her teeth to bite through the duct tape to free her mouth.

She remembered some years ago her family had all been given instruction by the F.B.I on the subject of kidnapping and hostage-taking. With her family being multimillionaires and in the public eye, there was always a chance of such a situation occurring. She had been told it would be in her best interests to know what to do. Now, more than ever, she was glad that she had paid attention to the instructions.

Amongst the valuable advice Ruby had been given were various methods of breaking and escaping bonds. She was so grateful that she had listened. Her jaw now ached, and her tongue was red raw from loosening the gag, but it had worked.

As her torso was being taped, she had also remembered another vital tip. If captured and you are going to be bound around the chest then, just before it happens, take a deep breath and inflate your chest. When it is taped, breathe out and you will find the bonds will not be completely tight. She had done this successfully, but her limbs were now the major problem.

Ruby had looked around the cellar which was mostly stocked with beer barrels. Some were connected to pumps to supply the bar upstairs, and many others were for stock. There was also crate upon crate of bottles of designer beer, lager, and cider, plus many boxes of wine.

She shuffled her chair forward towards the boxes of wine. She moved carefully, not wanting to topple the chair over. When she finally got there, she noticed that a Stanley knife was perched on top of an open box, with the blade still exposed. Whoever had used it last must have been in a hurry to get a bottle up to the bar and left it there undetected. What a stroke of luck.

She shuffled the chair around and edged it as close to the boxes as possible. She stretched her taped hands as wide as she could and, after three attempts, her fingers closed around the blade. She breathed a sigh of relief. Sweat sheened her forehead, partially from exhaustion and partially through fear of one of her capturers coming back.

She then began to manoeuvre the blade to cut through her bonds.

Suddenly, she heard raised voices from overhead, which she assumed was the main bar. It seemed like two men arguing. Then she heard a door open and footsteps on the stairs.

She shuffled herself back to the centre of the room and hung her head limply to her chest. She gripped the knife with all her might, hoping to God that whoever was coming would not check her bonds.

She heard a key in the lock of the cellar door, and it creaked open. Ruby remained still. She waited, praying whoever it was would not come any further. She then heard a voice shout down the stairs.

'Everything alright, Will?' Ruby recognised Keating's voice.

'Yeah. All good, Lenny. The bitch is asleep.'

'Right, lock it up and get back up here.'

The door shut and Ruby breathed out another sigh of relief. She immediately began to work on her bonds again.

In the bar upstairs, Joel Sterling downed a shot of whisky. He was still smarting from the argument he'd had with Keating. Joel had told his boss that he thought they should take off somewhere and lie low and regroup. In doing so, maybe this lunatic that was coming for the girl would back off. He could not understand why Keating wanted to stand his ground and fight this man.

Keating, though, had dismissed the idea immediately and told Joel he was not running anywhere. He was finishing it here and now. He told Joel he did not run from anybody. There were four of them and one of him. 'Get this joker out of the picture,' he had said, 'then the ransom deal can go ahead smoothly.'

Sterling had looked towards Big Will and 'Mad' Micky for support, but it was not forthcoming. They had bottled it.

As he helped himself to another scotch, Keating reappeared with Big Will. He addressed the three men.

'Right, the girl is asleep and locked up. So, let's get ready for "Rambo". If this all goes to plan, we stand to walk out of here and make some serious money. Enough to disappear on a plane to Barbados, Bali or Timbuktu, and live the high life. So, let's do this last job, okay?'

The men all produced their weapons. They all had Glock 17s except Micky, who was brandishing a Mossberg 500 12-gauge pump action shotgun.

'All quiet out the front, Micky?' asked Keating.

Micky nodded. 'Yes, boss.'

'Okay, keep an eye out.'

Keating looked at Big Will.

'Go out the back and check the car park area.'

The big man moved off without question.

'Joel, stay here in the bar.'

The younger man took a swallow of whisky and said nothing. For all his bravado, inside he was scared.

Big Will looked out of a rear window onto the club's car park. It was a flat gravelled area that had space for maybe fifty cars. At the moment, there were only four vehicles parked there. They all belonged to the men here. The light was fading as evening began to draw in. All seemed normal out there. He reached into his pocket for his cigarettes and headed to the fire exit door. He needed a quick smoke. It could not do any harm.

Tony Slade moved ahead cautiously. He picked up the scent of stale beer and rotten food coming from the dumpsters and empty beer barrels that were stacked halfway down the alley. This side of the club seemed to be solid brick wall. No windows were visible.

As he passed the dumpsters, the smell grew stronger. Rubbish had spewed out of them and was scattered all over the ground. Suddenly, something moved in the shadows, and Tony dropped into a fighting stance with the blade held tight in his rear hand.

A cat shot out from behind the dumpsters with what appeared to be a chicken bone in its mouth. It regarded Tony for a second and then ran off with its prey. Tony drew a deep breath and moved on. He could now see what looked like a car park opening out at the end of the alley. There was a fire door coming up on his right. Tony decided to see if, by any chance, it was open.

Just as he headed towards it, the door swung outward and a huge black man stepped out. He was in the process of lighting up a cigarette.

Big Will saw Tony standing there and instantly dropped the cigarette and lighter and reached inside his coat for his gun. Tony reacted faster and moved in close. He jammed the man's arm, and at the same time drove the knife into his stomach. The blade found its mark, slicing into the flesh like it was going through hot butter.

Tony kept driving in the blade as he pushed the man's huge bulk up against the wall. The big man shouted out in pain, but fought back by driving his hand into Tony's face, gouging at his eyes. Tony pulled the blade free and drove it in to the man's abdomen once again, this time twisting the blade. The big man stopped struggling.

Tony reached into the man's jacket and took his gun.
'How many are inside?' he asked.

Big Will gritted his teeth through the pain. His eyes were glazing over.

'Fuck you, man. I'm not telling you shit,' he whispered.

Tony pulled the blade out and Big Will slid down the wall to a seated position. Shock had set in from his wounds. Tony regarded him as he wiped the blade clean on an old beer towel he found in the rubbish strewn around the floor. He sheathed the blade then pointed the man's own gun at him.

'Last chance. I can still ring for a paramedic and they can save you. You don't need to die. So, I will ask you again. How many are inside?'

Big Will defiantly spat out a mouthful of blood.

'Fuck you, asshole. Your girl is going to die, and you won't be able to do jack shit. You're too late.'

Tony smiled grimly.

'We'll see.'

He walked past the dying man and moved towards the open fire door. He stole a quick glance in. He saw a dimly lit corridor leading, he presumed, into the bar. It was clear, so he went inside. As he did so, he heard the mobile phone of the man outside in the alley ringing.

The three men in the bar all exchanged nervous glances. Keating tried Big Will's mobile again. He let it ring a dozen times. No answer.

'Right, the bastard's here. Joel, go check on the girl. As long as we have her, we'll have some leverage over this Slade guy. She is our trump card.'

As Joel headed to the stairs, they all heard police sirens somewhere in the distance.

'Micky, hold him off here if you can. I need to sort something in the office.'

The man nodded in response and racked his shotgun.

Keating walked out the back into his office. On the wall, behind a hand-painted portrait of Bob Marley, was a safe. He worked the combination and it opened silently. Unzipping a large holdall, he emptied the contents of the safe into the bag. Huge bundles of cash, diamonds, and drugs went in. If everything was going tits up here, he needed a back-up plan in place, and the contents of this bag would help.

He realised that running was fruitless until he took this Slade character down, but if the odds were stacked against him, he was astute enough to get out of it and live to fight another day. He hadn't got to where he was without being resourceful. *Fuck the others! They would have to fend for themselves.* What they did not realise was that, just like the teenagers that Keating exploited for his drugs run, in the end they were also expendable.

With the tyre changed, Richmond and Drury sped to *Roxy's*. They killed the siren as they arrived. There was no sign of the firearms unit as yet.

Richmond pulled out his weapon and checked it. Then he returned it to the inside of his jacket. He now checked in the glove compartment for chewing gum. His mouth was dry. A by-product of adrenaline build-up.

'Luke, do me a favour and ring Bill Casper and see where he is. He should have been here by now.'

'Right, Gov.'

Drury knew exactly where Bill Casper was heading. The phone call he'd made whilst changing the tyre had been to direct Casper back to the *Raw Power* gym. He had apologised to Casper for the confusion and change of plan, but said it was due to them having been giving the wrong information.

Basically, Casper was not coming here any time soon, but Drury needed to go through the ploy of making the call until he could figure out his next step. But, by mistake, his next step materialised out of nowhere.

Preoccupied with his thoughts, Drury reached into his coat pocket and pulled out his mobile. He went to unlock it before, to his horror, he realised that he had pulled out Albert Sweet's mobile phone by mistake. In the heat of the moment, he had forgotten that he still had it.

He glanced in Richmond's direction, but there was no getting away from the fact that his boss had just clocked the distinctive red leather case. Time seemed to freeze in the car. Then Richmond spoke.

'What the fuck are you doing with that phone? It should be with Harriet Grey. No wonder she couldn't find it. What is going on, Luke?'

Richmond then saw the gun being levelled at him and it all began to make sense: how Keating's Range Rover had suddenly been reported as stolen; the missing phone; Sweet's death, how Keating always seemed to be one step ahead. It was because Sergeant Luke Drury had been supplying him with the information.

'Fuck, Luke. Why?'

'You wouldn't understand. It has all gone too far,' said the younger man, 'Now, slowly, with the two fingers of your left hand, get out your firearm and throw it onto the back seat.'

'Christ, Luke. You don't need to do this.'

Drury thrust his gun into Richmond's ribs.

'Just do it, Steve. Now. Then the same with your phone.'

Richmond did as he was told.

'Good. Now, get out of the car slowly,' instructed Drury.

Richmond got out.

'What are you going to do, Luke? Kill me? You will never get away with it.'

Drury laughed.

'Oh, I think I will. You just got caught in the crossfire of a gun battle here. Collateral damage. Nobody will be any the wiser. Now, get down that alleyway.'

Richmond walked slowly to the entrance.

'Bill Casper will be here any minute,' he argued. 'They will take you down.'

Drury laughed.

'Yeah. Funny thing about Casper. He got a call earlier, telling him there had been a change of plan and he was to go to the *Raw Power* gym instead. Strange that. Some mix-up in intel.'

Richmond's heart sank.

'Now get moving,' said Drury, as he prodded his superior in the back with the Glock.

Tony Slade tightly gripped the Glock 17 he had taken off the man outside, then he drew his own as well. He crept up to the double doors that stood in front of him. He didn't know what lay beyond them, but he had come this far, and Ruby was somewhere in the building. Whatever the outcome, he needed to save her. Maybe his whole life had come down to this defining moment. He stepped back, got his balance, and then kicked the doors wide open and entered firing.

'Turn around and back up against the wall,' instructed Drury.

Richmond raised his hands and slowly backed up.

'So, this is it, Luke. You're going to kill me here in this stinking alleyway in cold blood?'

'Just shut up and get against the wall,' shouted Drury.

'I don't think you have the cojones for it. It takes a lot of bottle to look a man in the face and shoot him.'

Drury was uncomfortably sweating in his suit.

'Maybe. Let's find out, shall we?' he replied.

Just then, both men heard the gunfire from inside the building. Just for a second, Drury's attention was drawn to the noise and he had taken his eyes off his boss. But DI Steve Richmond seized the moment. He swept the gun out of Drury's path and unloaded a right cross on his jaw. The younger man fell back, his legs collapsing under him. He was unconscious before he hit the ground.

Richmond shook his hand in pain. He was sure that a knuckle had broken. He reached down, took Drury's gun, and cautiously moved down the alleyway.

He passed the bled-out corpse of Big Will with a cursory glance then slipped inside the open fire door. Gunfire echoed around the building like a bad day in Afghanistan. His heart was beating like a trip hammer and his right hand was hurting like a bitch.

Tony fired across the room, his eyes scanning everywhere. He then caught sight of a man over by the far window levelling a shotgun at him. He ducked low as a 12-gauge shell tore a hole in the doorframe. Tony returned his fire, but the man was well concealed behind a stack of wooden tables and chairs.

The shotgun sounded again, blasting a piece out of the bar. Tony crawled on his belly behind it then popped up and unloaded a couple more rounds. The gun he had taken from Big Will was now empty. He dropped it to the floor.

A return shotgun blast exploded into the bar's optics, sending glass and alcohol everywhere. Tony emptied his own gun in the direction of the man, but with no luck. He then had an idea.

He reached out on the floor and picked up a bottle of whisky that had fallen from the shelf. He unscrewed the top and shoved a glass cleaning rag into the top. Reaching into his pocket, he produced a lighter and lit up the rag. Once it was burning strongly, he rose quickly and threw it in the direction of the man. The bottle exploded in a fire ball.

The heavy window drapes immediately caught fire, which in turn set Micky's whisky-soaked clothes instantly alight. He ran out from his cover, screaming in pain, but still managed to unload the shotgun in Tony's direction. As glass showered everywhere, Micky frantically beat himself, trying to put out the flames, and at the same time trying to reload. He then ignited into a fireball.

Tony crouched down and reloaded both guns. He then stood up and squeezed off two shots that hit the flaming figure squarely in the chest, and Micky went down.

Tony moved out from behind the bar and cautiously walked over to the downed man. The smell of burnt flesh reached his nostrils. It was nothing new to him. He had smelt it many times before in war.

He surveyed the room for others. It was empty.

Tony pulled another drape down from a window and covered it over the man, extinguishing the flames. He pulled the curtain off the body and looked down at it. Miraculously, the man was still breathing. His eyes were open, staring up at Tony. Through excruciating pain, he managed to say, 'Finish me, you bastard. Put me out of this fucking pain.'

Tony nodded. He pointed one of his guns downwards and put a round straight through the man's heart.

Chapter eighteen

Joel Sterling cowered at the bottom of the cellar stairs as the firefight above him suddenly stopped. He was way out of his depth. His bottle was being severely tested. Yes, he was no stranger to violence, but he was used to having the odds tipped in his favour. This was a completely different ball game. He did not want to die. He was only twenty-five years of age, for fuck's sake.

He needed to get out of here, and the best chance was to take the girl. If this Slade dude wanted her, then he could negotiate with him. Fuck Keating. It was every man for himself.

He opened the cellar door and moved into the room. The girl was still slumped in the chair. He moved closer to her.

'Alright, baby. Here's the deal. I'm going to undo your bonds and you're coming up the stairs with me. There just might be a chance that you're going home if you do exactly as I tell you. Understand?'

Ruby nodded subserviently.

As Joel leaned forward, Ruby, who had been successful in cutting through her bonds, waited for her chance then sprung up, slashing the Stanley blade across Joel's neck. He howled in pain and surprise, and dropped his gun as he clutched his neck, trying to stem the sudden flow of blood.

Ruby did not wait to see any more. She was running for the open door and the cellar steps.

As she reached the top of the stairs, she blinked in the sudden bright light. She was momentarily disorientated, and then she saw Tony Slade standing six feet or so away, directly in front of her, pointing a gun. She raised her hands in fear.

'Drop to your knees right now, Ruby. No questions. Go!'

She did what she was told and gave Tony a clear shot as a blood-drenched Joel Sterling staggered to the top step of the stairs, one hand still clamped hopelessly to his neck and the other trying to level his gun. Tony fired, blowing the man's face off. His body disappeared back down the stairs.

Ruby screamed, then picked herself up and ran into Tony's arms. She clutched him tightly.

'It's okay. I've got you now. It's going to be alright.' Easing her away from his body, he saw blood on her clothes and hands. 'Are you hurt?'

'No, it's not mine. I'm fine.'

Tony breathed a sigh of relief. He then clicked back on.

'Keating is still in here somewhere. I'm going to finish this. I need you to get out of here and phone the police.'

Suddenly, a voice broke the silence.

'No need. They're already here. Hello, Slade. Long time and all that.'

Tony turned around to see DI Richmond in the doorway, pointing a gun directly at him.

'Drop the weapons, Slade.'

Tony did as instructed.

Richmond gestured to Ruby. 'Move away from Slade, Ms Carter. I suggest you come over towards me.'

Ruby looked at Tony.

'Do as he says, Ruby.'

Richmond smiled and Ruby slowly walked towards the policeman.

'Sensible move, Slade. You know that I have dreamt of finally getting another chance to come face-to-face with you again. Once I found out that you were the girl's father, I had a feeling that you would come out of hiding if I brought her to the UK. And, well, here you are.'

'Well, give yourself a pat on the back, why don't you?' replied Slade.

Richmond shook his head in dismay.

'Always the joker, Slade. Right up to the end. You know I'm not here to take you in. No, it's all going to end right here and now.'

'So, you're going to murder me here, in front of a witness who happens to be my daughter, are you?' asked Tony.

Richmond regarded Ruby.

'Who said anything about witnesses?'

Tony moved forward. 'You bastard, Richmond.'

The DI levelled his gun.

'Stay fucking still, Slade or I will—'

The air suddenly echoed with another gunshot. The white shirt that Richmond had been wearing under his suit jacket turned red. He dropped to his knees and then forward, face down. Standing behind him with his gun still smoking was Sergeant Luke Drury.

After regaining consciousness, Drury had gone back to the police car and retrieved his governor's gun from the back seat. Then he had made his way inside the club just in time for Richmond's speech.

Keating heard the gunfire cease. He exited his office and entered the cellar through another door. Once inside, he found the empty chair where the girl had sat. On closer inspection, he found blood over the chair and floor. A trail of it led to the cellar door which stood ajar.

Moving towards it, he opened the door fully and nearly tripped over the dead body of Joel Sterling. He regarded the man dispassionately. He now could only suspect that Micky and Will had also been taken out. This Slade dude was good.

As Keating crept up the stairs, another gunshot sounded, and then he heard a voice he recognised. Sergeant Luke Drury. He placed the holdall on a step, drew his gun, and moved silently to the top of the stairs.

Ruby ran back to Slade and clung to him. She then turned to Drury.

'I don't understand why you shot your own boss.'

Drury brought the gun down.

'He was dirty. I've suspected it for a while. He's been on Keating's payroll for some time, taking backhanders for information. He's been tampering with this case from day one. That's why Keating knew of your whereabouts at the hotel. He tipped him off.'

He regarded Slade.

'Richmond certainly had a hard-on for you, Slade. Obsessed would be the best way to describe it. He was fervent when he knew you fell for his bait. I guess I did you a favour.'

Slade looked at Drury.

'So, what now?'

'You can both go. I have no beef with you, Slade. You can go back to where you came from. As far as I'm concerned, you were never here.'

He looked around the room then raised an eyebrow.

'Keating?'

'Still here somewhere, unless he has legged it.'

At that moment, Keating rose from his hiding place, his gun levelled.

'Amazing story, Drury. You should get an Oscar for that acting.'

Before Drury could bring his gun up, Keating had fired off two rounds. The first bullet tore into the policeman's shoulder, sending him staggering back against the wall. The second one hit the doorframe above his head.

Drury fired off a shot at Keating, which seared pass his head, taking the tip off his right ear. Keating moved into the room and unloaded his gun until the clip was empty. Drury dropped in a hail of bullets as they tore through his vital organs.

As this was happening, Tony Slade seized his chance and ushered Ruby towards the cellar steps and safety. He could not afford the chance of a firefight in the open, with his daughter exposed. Her safety was paramount.

'Go to the cellar and lock the door. Don't open it until I come and tell you.'

'Please, Tony. I don't want to leave you,' sobbed Ruby.

'Do it now, Ruby. We have no time.'

She moved down the stairs as Tony pulled the CZ 75B from his coat.

'I don't want to lose you as well, Tony. Please be careful.'

Tony nodded and watched her turn her face away from the body of Joel Sterling, enter the cellar, and shut the door. He moved back up to the top of the stairs. Everything was quiet.

The atmosphere of the room hung heavy with the smell of cordite and something else – death.

Tony scanned around. It looked like a scene straight out of an old Wild West movie after a saloon shoot-out. Where the fuck was Keating?

A movement to his right alerted him, but he was not quick enough to stop Keating's heavy bulk slamming into him and knocking him off his feet. Tony's gun went flying out of his hands. He hit the ground hard with Keating on top of him.

Tony was no stranger to fighting on the floor, as he was a Jujutsu black belt, but his sixty-year-old body felt the impact hard. He was winded badly.

Keating was a steroid monster with incredible power, and he began to rain blows down on Tony's head. Tony covered up and manoeuvred his body so that he could wrap his legs around Keating's waist and pull him down into the classic Jujutsu 'guard' position.

He wrapped up Keating's arms, and headbutted him squarely on the nose. The big man grunted and leant in, attempting to bite Tony's ear. Tony stopped him with a well-timed thumb gouge into the big man's left eye socket.

Keating pulled back and ripped himself free. He slid his left arm under Tony's right leg in an attempt to get past it. Tony immediately seized the chance to wrap his right leg around and behind Keating's neck, and then joined his foot in a tight lock behind his left knee.

He now had Keating in what was termed a 'triangle leg choke'. He pulled down on the big man's head and squeezed his thighs together, beginning to cut the blood flow off to the brain. This was a powerful and highly effective strangle, known as *sangaku-jime* in Jujutsu and Judo.

He remembered his old mentor and instructor Ray Steele putting him to sleep in this hold on the training mats, way back when Tony had been an eager eighteen-year-old novice. After the experience, he had asked Ray what he had done and to show him it. Later, it became a favourite signature move of his.

Tony kept squeezing. Keating's eyes were bulging from the sockets and his breathing was laboured, but he was still gamely in the fight. Using an incredible reserve of strength, he lifted Tony up from the floor – with him still wrapped around his neck – and then slammed him down onto a wooden trestle table.

The impact was huge. It took the air completely out of Tony and shook him up as the table exploded into pieces. He was forced to release his hold.

With Keating back on top of him, he once again fended off the wild swinging punches, but caught a headbutt full in the face that bloodied his nose and made his eyes water profusely. Tony's body was now feeling the rigours of combat. He was breathing heavily.

Keating might not have his technical fighting skills, but he was younger and stronger.

As the two men continued to struggle. Tony felt Keating's hand reach around his back to find his knife. He grabbed at the arm to stop it, but Keating had already released the blade.

He jabbed it into Tony's side and the blade sank in two inches or so. The adrenaline masked the majority of the pain, but now he was at a distinct disadvantage on the floor.

Keating now sat back and raised the knife above his head in a two-handed ice-pick grip. Tony immediately opened the grip he had with his legs around Keating's waist and shuffled backwards quickly, using both his feet to kick the big man in the chest and send him backwards. Keating's head hit a bar stool which momentarily stunned him.

Tony got to his knees and saw the pump action shotgun lying on the ground where 'Mad' Micky had dropped it. There were shells scattered on the floor where the man had frantically tried to reload.

He grabbed the gun, picked up a shell, and fed it into the chamber, praying that it would fire. Tony's hands were shaking and slippery with blood, which did not make loading easy.

As he turned to face Keating, he found the big man was nearly on him, blade raised once more for the kill. Tony thrust a front kick into his adversary's stomach, bringing the man to an abrupt halt, then levelled the gun and pulled the trigger. The shell blasted a hole in the chest of Keating, who staggered back but still stood brandishing the knife.

Tony ran at him. As he did, he flipped the gun over and swung the stock of it in a vicious arc that smashed into Keating's temple. This time, the big man went and the knife slipped from his fingers. Tony reached down, picked it up, and drove it to the hilt into Keating's neck. The big man's eyes rolled over white as the life drained out of him.

Tony touched his fingers to the pulse in Keating's neck. He could feel none. He retrieved his knife, returning it to its sheath.

He now felt the wound in his own side. It wasn't serious. He would patch it up when he got back to his car. There was a first aid kit in the boot.

Tony walked wearily down the cellar steps and knocked on the door.

'Ruby. It's me. You can unlock the door. It's safe.'

He heard the key turn in the lock, and the door tentatively opened to reveal Ruby's worried features. When she saw it was Tony, she rushed into his arms sobbing.

He held her tight. He could feel her heart beating against his chest. A deep feeling of love rushed into his body that had been dormant since Annette's death. It was a feeling he'd thought he would never experience ever again. Tony smoothed her hair and spoke softly.

'It's okay, Ruby. It's all over now. You're safe.'

Ruby looked up into his face.

'I'm sorry it came to this. I should have listened to you. I never thought in a million years that Keating would come looking for me.'

'Forget it, Ruby. What's done is done. Let's get out of here. More police are bound to be on their way, and I don't want to be around to explain this mess.'

As they walked up the stairs, Tony spied the holdall that Keating had left there. On opening it, he let out a low whistle at the contents. He pulled out the bags of cocaine and disregarded them.

'What are you going to do with the rest of the contents?' asked Ruby.

'Well, nobody here has a use for it, but I am sure I can find one. Trust me, I seem to have an affinity with holdalls full of money.' As Tony passed Richmond's body he bent down and picked up something from the floor and slipped it in his pocket.

Outside, they passed the body of Big Will, where the carnage had started. Ruby averted her eyes. Tony put his arm around her and guided her out of the alleyway and back to where his vehicle was parked. He opened the boot and threw the bag in, then they got into the car.

Tony shoved the keys into the ignition, ready to start the engine. He glanced over at Ruby. She looked so vulnerable. Almost childlike. He reached out and touched her cheek. She smiled and squeezed his hand.

'So, what now, Dad? You sure picked one hell of a way for us to get to know each other.'

Tony laughed. 'You don't say."

His face became more serious.

"You need to get to the police and tell them you managed to get away. Tell them you escaped from the bar cellar after you heard a gun battle going on upstairs. When you got out, everybody was dead, so you just ran for it. They have nothing on you whatsoever. You are the victim in this mess. Then, when it is sorted, get back to New York and safety."

He fished in his pocket and produced her mobile phone.

"Here you go, you can have this back now. That was a very clever move keeping the connection open in the shower."

Ruby's took the phone.

"I knew you would come for me."

She added, 'Come back to the States with me for a while. You can visit Mum. I'm sure she would love to see you. It would be a tonic for her.'

Tony felt an uncertainty rise in his body.

'I don't know, Ruby. That's a big step. Things have moved so fast...'

Ruby touched his arm.

'I'm sorry. This isn't the time or place to suggest that. Particularly after all that's happened. It's just that now I've found you, I don't want to lose you. Just promise me one thing, that you'll think about it?'

Tony leant over and kissed her cheek.

'I promise. Now I know where you are, I don't want to lose you either. But for the moment I need to make myself scarce and tie up a few loose ends. After that, I'll call you and we will see where we go from there. How does that sound?"

Ruby smiled. "That sounds like a plan."

Tony went to pull on his seat belt and then stopped.

'Shit!' he exclaimed.

'What is it?' asked Ruby.

'The guns I used. I need to get them. I promised a friend. I can't let the police seize them. I won't be long. If anybody turns up when I am gone, start the car and get away.'

'Please hurry, Tony, and be careful,' said Ruby.

As he got out of the car, he turned back towards her and, in his best Terminator voice, said, 'I'll be back.'

Ruby gave him a weak smile and watched him until he disappeared back into the alleyway. She could hear the distant sound of sirens getting closer. She shifted into the driver's seat and started the ignition, drumming her fingertips nervously on the steering wheel.

Tony made his way back into the club. Big Will's body was now attracting flies.

Walking into the bar, everything was deadly silent. It was dark and gloomy as the evening light was fading. Tony quickly moved to the far side of the room and, with little trouble, found the CZ which had flown out of his hand when Keating had attacked him.

Now, he moved back towards the centre and picked up his Glock. He holstered both guns. Finally, he retrieved Big Will's gun and wiped it clean of prints on an old tablecloth then jammed it in his waistband. He would drop it by the man's body on the way out of the building. He then decided to rip off a piece of the cloth to use as a makeshift padding to stem the flow of blood from his wound.

He did one final check.

The shotgun man's dead body was still smouldering There was one body at the bottom of the cellar steps. Keating lay at the bar. Tony walked towards the door and regarded the bloodied body of Luke Drury. Such a young man to die so violently. One of many he had seen over the years.

Then he froze. *How the fuck did he miss it on the way in?* He'd been too preoccupied with finding his guns. *What a fool.* The body of DI Steve Richmond was not where it had been lying earlier. By the time this cold realisation hit him, he felt the hard tip of a gun at the back of his head.

'Don't move a fucking muscle, Slade.'

Richmond's voice was rasping, and his breathing laboured.

'I knew I would fucking get you in the end. What a stroke of luck you came back. I don't think I have much more time or strength left in me. I have lost a lot of blood, but I have just enough life left in me for this. Now, get on your fucking knees slowly.'

Tony felt an icy finger of cold sweat trickle down his spine as he began to lower himself.

Richmond laughed.

'Not such a smartass now are we Slade?'

Before Tony could reply, Detective Sergeant Steve Richmond pulled the trigger.

Epilogue

Ruby heard gunshots and a coldness spread through her body. She flung open the car door, got out, and ran back towards the club and the alleyway, just as a cavalcade of police vehicles sped around the corner to grind to a halt outside *Roxy's*. Armed police jumped out of vans.

Ruby was momentarily confused at what to do. She went into a panic.

Then she heard her name being called and turned to see P.C. Debbie Garrett.

The policewoman walked towards her.

'Ruby, thank God you are safe. Are you hurt?'

Ruby ignored the question.

'I heard gunshots... I have to go back in... I need...' She stumbled over her words.

P.C. Garrett wrapped a protective arm around her shoulders.

'It's ok. It's over. You're safe. Let the police sort it now. The main thing is that you got away."

Ruby looked towards the alleyway.

'No. You don't understand... He came to save me... He went back in... He said he didn't want to lose me..."

P.C. Garrett looked confused.

'Who are you talking about Ruby? Who went back in?'

Ruby looked into the questioning eyes of the policewoman. 'My dad, of course."

P.C. Garrett saw the look of concern and anxiety on Ruby's face.

'Your father passed away, Ruby. He was in a car accident, remember?'

Ruby became agitated.

'No. My real father. He went back inside. There were gunshots. I have to get to him.'

Ruby struggled to move away from the other woman's grip, but she couldn't.

'Wait, Ruby. You are not making sense. Calm down a moment.'

Suddenly the realisation hit her, and P.C. Garrett understood.

'Ruby. Do you mean Tony Slade?'

'Yes. Yes. Please let me go.'

'No Ruby. I can't let you go back inside. It is too dangerous. The armed response team will bring out whoever is left inside."

Ruby slumped against the car. Fatigue enveloped her body. Her shoulders drooped in resignation. Then the tears came. The whole aftermath of the ordeal she had gone through began to manifest itself.

P.C. Garrett glanced across the road as the paramedics arrived. She gestured for them to attend to Ruby.

'The paramedics will take care of you now, Ruby. We'll talk later.'

Ruby didn't answer. Shock was setting into her body.

P.C. Garrett watched as she was led away. She was still trying to process the conversation they had just had. *Was Tony Slade really inside the club?*

......

Superintendent Hardwick and Detective Sergeant Bob Pritchard walked out of the alley.

'What a fucking bloodbath, sir. Haven't seen anything like that in all my years on the force,' said Pritchard.

'Yes, quite, Sergeant. A right mess. The press will have a field day,' replied Hardwick.

Then, as an afterthought, he added, 'Bloody tragic to lose two of our boys. But at least they lost their lives for a noble cause, bringing down a notorious drug dealer and saving a high-profile hostage. Probably be a commendation in it somewhere for them."

D.S. Pritchard took a drag on his cigarette and regarded his boss; Hardwick never failed to amaze him.

'I am sure that will be a big fucking consolation to their families, sir.' He walked off before Hardwick could reply.

Pritchard joined P.C. Garrett, shaking his head.

'That Harddick is a right fucking piece of work,' he grumbled.

Garrett laughed.

'Already worrying about the political ramifications, no doubt.'

Pritchard dropped the butt of his cigarette and crushed it out with the sole of his shoe.

'You got it. It's a right bastard losing Richmond and Drury. But they went out in a blaze of glory. Christ knows what went on in that club. It looked like a scene from *Full Metal Jacket*.'

The reference to the war film prompted Debbie Garrett to ask, 'Sir, did they find the body of Tony Slade in there? I fancy a lot of what went down in there could be his handiwork.'

Pritchard looked surprised.

'You mean *the* elusive Tony Slade that Richmond obsessed over? Why the hell would he be involved in this? Wait, hang on, there was a story in the newspaper about him being her dad, right? Did the girl say he was in there?'

'I'm not sure. She seems confused and in shock. She didn't really make sense.'

'So, what other suspicions have you got, Garrett? Come on, enlighten me.'

Garrett explained that Luke Drury had confided in her about Richmond's plan to get Slade out of hiding by bringing his daughter, Ruby Carter, to the UK, and how Drury had been worried that his boss was fixated with this rather than looking for the killers of Gary Carter. She had eventually gone to Hardwick with this information, who immediately tried to track down Richmond, and then eventually unravelled the trail that had led them all to the final crime scene. It looked like Richmond had been holding out on other members of the team and had been following his own agenda.

Pritchard listened with interest until Garrett finished.

'Well, fucking hell. All this was happening when I left the original case. What a crafty bastard Richmond was. He had me fooled. I had no idea.'

He stepped closer to P.C. Garrett. 'Do you know what this Slade character looked like?'

'No, I have only seen a newspaper image of him when he was a young paratrooper.'

Pritchard looked over towards the paramedics.

'I bet I know someone who does, though.'

Garrett followed his gaze towards Ruby Carter, who was sitting on the back step of the ambulance. She had a blanket draped around her shoulders, and she was sipping water as she was being checked over.

'Gov, don't you think she has been through enough? She has lost one father and a brother already. How much more can one person take?' If Slade is amongst the body count, I think it will tip her over the edge.'

'That is true, Garrett, but Harddick is the officer in charge here, so it's his decision.'

'Only if you tell him, Gov.'

'I'll pretend I didn't hear that, Police Constable,' replied Pritchard, as he walked away towards Superintendent Hardwick.

Ruby watched the chaotic scene going on around her, and her mind went back over what had happened in the club while she estimated the body count in her head. Four bad guys and two crooked policemen. That made six, minus Tony.

She waited, her heart hammering in her chest. She clasped her hands in a silent prayer.

Bob Casper and his team suddenly appeared from the alleyway of the club.

Casper looked towards Superintendent Hardwick.

'That's it, sir. All clear. Six bodies in total. All dead on our arrival. When the SOCO boys arrive, it's all theirs.'

Ruby heard what he said and her legs almost buckled under her. Relief flooded through her body.

She then saw the senior policeman approach her.

'Ms Carter,' Hardwick began, 'I realise what a harrowing experience you have been through and also the tragic circumstances you have been dealing with of late, but I want to ask you to please help us wrap up this case, if you can.'

Ruby remained silent and Hardwick continued.

'I understand from information I received that D.I. Richmond believed Tony Slade was coming here to save you. Was he in the club when you escaped?'

Ruby suddenly felt afraid and instantly regretted what she had said to the WPC earlier. She needed to think of something fast.

'I don't know. I escaped from the cellar I was being held in, and ran straight out here. There were bodies everywhere. I had heard a massive gun battle going on whilst I was captive, but I didn't see exactly who was involved. I was disorientated and frightened. I just wanted to escape.'

'Yes. Of course. I understand. It must have been terrible for you. But I need to ask you this. You probably know the police have been looking to speak with Tony Slade for some while over more than one important matter. To close the book on him, we need to identify his body, and unfortunately you are the only person present that can do that. I know you have been through so much, but it would help us out greatly."

Ruby drew in a large breath and replied, 'Ok. If you think he is in there, I will do it. I need closure on this myself.'

Superintendent Hardwick nodded. 'Thank you, Ms Carter.'

D.S. Pritchard, who had been standing in the background listening, came forward.

'Ms Carter. This is going to be a quick and straightforward procedure. We have identified all the bodies in the club except one. A white male. And I must warn you that the body is quite severely burnt. We don't immediately recognise him, so there is a strong possibility that it is Slade.'

'Thank you, Sergeant,' answered Hardwick.

'If you are ready, Ms Carter, then please follow me.'

Ruby followed Hardwick back down the alleyway towards the fire doors.

'Please be warned, there are some pretty distressing scenes inside and outside,' he told her.

A policeman stood guard at the door. He positioned himself to shield the body of Big Will from Ruby's gaze.

Once inside the bar of the club, the Superintendent led Ruby over to a body.

Hardwick spoke solemnly as they stopped in front of it. 'In your own time.'

Ruby was disgusted by the sight of the body, even though she could see it wasn't Tony. She played the frightened and apprehensive daughter as she stared down into the charred features of Mad Micky Stone – one of her captors.

She gasped and put her hand to her mouth.

'Is this the body of Tony Slade?' asked Hardwick.

Ruby hoped she looked suitably distraught when she answered, 'Yes, Superintendent, it is.'

They both regarded the badly charred features.

'You are positive, Ms Carter?' he urged.

'Yes, as far as I can tell. I only met this man in the last few days, but I am sure it is him.'

'The body is hardly recognisable, Ms Carter. How can you so sure?' pressed the Superintendent.

Ruby thought quickly.

'The gold chain around his neck. I recognise it. He wore it every time I met him. He told me it was special to him.

Hardwick took her arm gently and led her away.

'Thank you. I realise that couldn't have been easy for you.'

Ruby dabbed her eyes with a tissue.

'I would like to go back to my hotel now, please. I feel very tired.'

'Of course. I will organise you a lift. I will contact you tomorrow about coming in and giving us your full statement of what happened here today. For the moment, though, it can wait.'

Back outside the front of the club, Hardwick signalled to P.C. Debbie Garrett.

'Can you please organise a car and drive Ms Carter back to her hotel?"

'Yes, sir, I will sort it straight away.'

Hardwick walked back over to the police officers gathered around their vehicles.

'Ok, chaps. You are done here. Good job. You can get on your way. I will tie up any loose ends here with Sergeant Pritchard and wait for SOCO.'

Pritchard approached Hardwick.

'The girl positive of the I.D.?' he asked.

'As you said, the body is pretty severely burnt, but she seemed sure. Forensics may be able to confirm through dental records.'

'So, not only did we take down a drug gang, but we also nailed the fugitive Tony Slade.'

'Seems we did.'

'A good result all in all then, sir.'

'Yes, Sergeant, we can now draw a line under both matters and move on. The loss of two dedicated officers was not in vain.'

....

On the car journey back to the hotel, Ruby was lost deep in her thoughts. Tony was alive. She was sure of that. *But how did he get away? And where was he?*

The last month of her life had been crazy. So much had happened. It was going to take her some time to process everything that had gone on.

P.C. Garrett's voice eventually broke the silence.

'Here we are, Ruby. Home, safe and sound.'

Ruby gathered her thoughts.

'Thank you. I really appreciate all you have done.'

'No problem. Although this isn't a typical day in Bristol, England, I'll have you know.'

Ruby managed a weak smile and made to get out of the car.

'Oh, Ruby. Can I ask you something?' said P.C. Garrett.

'Yes, sure, what is it?"

'When I first saw you back at the club, you said to me Tony Slade went back inside.'

'Did I? I can't remember. I must have been in shock.'

'You were very adamant about this. You wanted to go in and find him.'

Ruby remained silent. She didn't like the way this conversation was heading.

P.C. Garrett continued, 'Well, if that was the case, it must have been something important to draw him back in there. I mean, he must have just got you out of an extremely dangerous situation. You were both in one piece. Why risk going back in? It ultimately cost him his life, didn't it?'

Ruby swallowed hard, letting tears well up in her eyes.

'Like I said, I was confused. I had just gone through a very traumatic time.'

P.C. Garrett nodded. 'Strange thing his death, don't you think?'

Ruby felt a sick feeling in her stomach.

'How do you mean?'

'Well, I remember you telling me you heard gunshots when he supposedly went back into the club, and then we were pretty much right there on the scene and went in ourselves.'

'Where are you going with this?' Ruby asked.

'I was just wondering how his body that you identified got burnt so badly in that short time?. This all seemed to happen pretty fast, don't you think?'

Ruby began to feel panic rising inside.

'I am sorry,' she said, 'but I have had enough today. I am so tired I can't think straight. All I know is I found somebody who I didn't know existed a short time ago, and now he has been taken away from me, just like other members of my family.'

P.C. Garrett studied Ruby. She looked shattered physically and mentally. The woman had been to hell and back.

'I am sorry, Ruby. It was insensitive of me to question you like that at this moment. Forgive me. It is the nature of the job. I have never wanted to be anything other than a police officer. It runs in the family. Grandfather and my dad.' She paused briefly then went on, 'I lost my dad in the line of duty, Ruby. I was only ten years old when he was shot and killed in a botched robbery on a building society.

'He was a good father and a good copper, and I still miss him. I can understand a little of what you are going through, believe me.'

Ruby nodded.

'Thank you. I didn't plan for all this to happen. I came here to bring my brother back home. Meeting my dad was totally unexpected. But I can tell you one thing, hand on heart, I wouldn't be alive if he hadn't come looking for me. The police certainly didn't do a great job on that front.'

P.C. Garrett couldn't argue with her.

'Fair enough. Look, Ruby. This is off the record, and you must never repeat this to anybody, understand?'

Ruby cautiously agreed. 'OK. What is it?'

'Only I know about the conversation we had about Tony going back into the club. Now, if he never came out of there with you in the first place, then the pieces fit to how we found the body. So, his death would not be deemed as suspicious. Plus, the body was so severely burnt I don't think the forensics people will be able to make a positive I.D. So, it will be down to your identification and yours alone.' Garrett paused. 'Do you understand what I am saying? Maybe you did get confused with the timing. Shock can do that. You have yet to give your full statement to the Superintendent, and I have still to write up my notes, so it would be easy for us to forget we had that conversation altogether.'

Ruby let the words sink in.

She leant over and gave the Constable a hug and whispered thank you in her ear.

As the car drove off, Ruby stood at the entrance to the hotel and breathed a huge sigh of relief. She had a feeling that things were going to work out alright.

As she walked up the steps and into the foyer, her mobile rang. She checked the caller I.D. and answered it immediately.

'Tony? Dad. Holy crap. What happened? Are you hurt? Where the hell are you now?'

Tony Slade was sitting in his hire car in a layby near Nailsea. In the boot, safely tucked away, were his weapons ready to be disposed of. He was on his way to pay off Eddie Montgomery Also safe in the boot was Keating's holdall of money and diamonds for a rainy day.

It had been a close thing back at the club with Richmond.

But Tony Slade had trained for those situations. He had stared death in the face more than once. His unarmed combat skills had been honed by countless hours dealing with how to defend against all manner of weapons.

As instructed, he had begun to slowly lower to his knees, then he'd suddenly dropped fast. His move had surprised Richmond, so when he pulled the trigger, his bullet missed and whizzed harmlessly over Slade's head.

As Tony fell, he pulled Big Will's gun from his waistband, spun over onto his back, and fired a shot straight between Richmond's eyes. The policeman was dead before he hit the ground.

Tony heard the sirens closing in; the way he had entered the building was no longer an escape option. He decided to avoid the cellar, in case there was no exit, so headed upstairs.

He had eventually found a trapdoor in the ceiling on the top floor that led him out onto the roof.

Tony began to shimmy across it like Spiderman. Being an ex-paratrooper meant he had no fear of heights.

From a vantage point on the roof, he watched the scene unfold below. He could make out Ruby talking to a policewoman. Knowing she was now safe, he headed across the wide expanse of tiles until he reached an iron ladder attached to the side of the building.

He tested it to see how secure it was by vigorously shaking it. It seemed solid enough. Tony climbed out on to it and began his descent.

Five minutes later, he had circled back undetected into the park, and carried on watching the scene unfold through the binoculars he had left in the bushes. Eventually, he saw the paramedics and the armed response team leave, followed shortly by Ruby with the policewoman.

As things died down, he took a casual walk back to his car and was relieved to see it was still there, with the keys left in the ignition. He had driven away undetected. Job done.

He smiled now as he heard Ruby's voice still questioning him frantically.

'Well, tell me, goddamit. What happened to you?'

Tony Slade leaned back in his seat and replied, 'Hold on a minute, Ruby, which one of those questions would you like me to answer first?'

About the Author

This is Kevin's third work of fiction.

His first novel was *Battlescars* (2018), in which he introduced readers to the character of Tony Slade. His second novel, *No Hiding Place* (2019), continued the story. Now, *Last Stand* gives us a trilogy of Slade adventures.

As well as being an author, Kevin is a globally renowned and respected martial artist. He has trained and taught for some 45 years.

While training, he started to write articles for martial arts magazines, which spurred him on to write a series of self-defence and combative instruction books. In 2017, he published his autobiography, *When We Were Warriors*. But his real passion is to write fiction.

Kevin lives in Bristol, UK, with his wife Tina. He is a father and grandfather.

He is now semi-retired from teaching martial arts, and spends his leisure time reading, writing, playing guitar, and travelling.